CYMBELINE (Large Print)

by

William Shakespeare (1564-1616)

Published 2018 by Literary Domain Publishing

ISBN-13: 978-1717269904

ISBN-10: 1717269907

CYMBELINE (Large Print)

by

William Shakespeare

Plot summary on page 173.

Cymbeline

ACT I. SCENE I. Britain. The garden of Cymbeline's palace.

Enter two Gentlemen

First Gentleman: You do not meet a man but frowns: our bloods No more obey the heavens than our courtiers
Still seem as does the king.

Second Gentleman: But what's the matter?

First Gentleman: His daughter, and the heir of's kingdom, whom He purposed to his wife's sole son--a widow
That late he married--hath referr'd herself
Unto a poor but worthy gentleman: she's wedded;
Her husband banish'd; she imprison'd: all
Is outward sorrow; though I think the king
Be touch'd at very heart.

Second Gentleman: None but the king?

First Gentleman: He that hath lost her too; so is the queen,
That most desired the match; but not a courtier,
Although they wear their faces to the bent
Of the king's look's, hath a heart that is not
Glad at the thing they scowl at.

Second Gentleman: And why so?

First Gentleman: He that hath miss'd the princess is a thing
Too bad for bad report: and he that hath her--
I mean, that married her, alack, good man!
And therefore banish'd--is a creature such
As, to seek through the regions of the earth
For one his like, there would be something failing
In him that should compare. I do not think
So fair an outward and such stuff within
Endows a man but he.

Second Gentleman: You speak him far.

First Gentleman: I do extend him, sir, within himself,
Crush him together rather than unfold
His measure duly.

Second Gentleman: What's his name and birth?

First Gentleman: I cannot delve him to the root: his father
Was call'd Sicilius, who did join his honour
Against the Romans with Cassibelan,
But had his titles by Tenantius whom
He served with glory and admired success,
So gain'd the sur-addition Leonatus;
And had, besides this gentleman in question,
Two other sons, who in the wars o' the time
Died with their swords in hand; for which
their father, Then old and fond of issue, took such sorrow
That he quit being, and his gentle lady,

Big of this gentleman our theme, deceased
As he was born. The king he takes the babe
To his protection, calls him Posthumus Leonatus,
Breeds him and makes him of his bed-chamber,
Puts to him all the learnings that his time
Could make him the receiver of; which he took,
As we do air, fast as 'twas minister'd,
And in's spring became a harvest, lived in court--
Which rare it is to do--most praised, most loved,
A sample to the youngest, to the more mature
A glass that feated them, and to the graver
A child that guided dotards; to his mistress,
For whom he now is banish'd, her own price
Proclaims how she esteem'd him and his virtue;
By her election may be truly read
What kind of man he is.

Second Gentleman: I honour him
Even out of your report. But, pray you, tell me,
Is she sole child to the king?

First Gentleman: His only child.
He had two sons: if this be worth your hearing,
Mark it: the eldest of them at three years old,
I' the swathing-clothes the other, from their nursery
Were stol'n, and to this hour no guess in knowledge
Which way they went.

Second Gentleman: How long is this ago?

First Gentleman: Some twenty years.

Second Gentleman: That a king's children should be so convey'd, So slackly guarded, and the search so slow, That could not trace them!

First Gentleman: Howsoe'er 'tis strange,
Or that the negligence may well be laugh'd at,
Yet is it true, sir.

Second Gentleman: I do well believe you.

First Gentleman: We must forbear: here comes the gentleman, The queen, and princess.

Exeunt

Enter the QUEEN, POSTHUMUS LEONATUS, and IMOGEN

QUEEN: No, be assured you shall not find me, daughter,
After the slander of most stepmothers,
Evil-eyed unto you: you're my prisoner, but
Your gaoler shall deliver you the keys
That lock up your restraint. For you, Posthumus,
So soon as I can win the offended king,
I will be known your advocate: marry, yet
The fire of rage is in him, and 'twere good
You lean'd unto his sentence with what patience
Your wisdom may inform you.

POSTHUMUS LEONATUS: Please your highness,
I will from hence to-day.

QUEEN: You know the peril.
I'll fetch a turn about the garden, pitying
The pangs of barr'd affections, though the king
Hath charged you should not speak together.

Exit

IMOGEN: O Dissembling courtesy! How fine this tyrant
Can tickle where she wounds! My dearest husband,
I something fear my father's wrath; but nothing--
Always reserved my holy duty--what
His rage can do on me: you must be gone;
And I shall here abide the hourly shot
Of angry eyes, not comforted to live,
But that there is this jewel in the world
That I may see again.

POSTHUMUS LEONATUS: My queen! my mistress!
O lady, weep no more, lest I give cause
To be suspected of more tenderness
Than doth become a man. I will remain
The loyal'st husband that did e'er plight troth:
My residence in Rome at one Philario's,
Who to my father was a friend, to me
Known but by letter: thither write, my queen,
And with mine eyes I'll drink the words you send,
Though ink be made of gall.

Re-enter QUEEN

QUEEN: Be brief, I pray you:
If the king come, I shall incur I know not
How much of his displeasure.

Aside

Yet I'll move him
To walk this way: I never do him wrong,
But he does buy my injuries, to be friends;
Pays dear for my offences.

Exit

POSTHUMUS LEONATUS: Should we be taking leave
As long a term as yet we have to live,
The loathness to depart would grow. Adieu!

IMOGEN: Nay, stay a little:
Were you but riding forth to air yourself,
Such parting were too petty. Look here, love;
This diamond was my mother's: take it, heart;
But keep it till you woo another wife,
When Imogen is dead.

POSTHUMUS LEONATUS: How, how! another?
You gentle gods, give me but this I have,
And sear up my embracements from a next

With bonds of death!

Putting on the ring

Remain, remain thou here
While sense can keep it on. And, sweetest, fairest,
As I my poor self did exchange for you,
To your so infinite loss, so in our trifles
I still win of you: for my sake wear this;
It is a manacle of love; I'll place it
Upon this fairest prisoner.

Putting a bracelet upon her arm

IMOGEN: O the gods!
When shall we see again?

Enter CYMBELINE and Lords

POSTHUMUS LEONATUS: Alack, the king!

CYMBELINE: Thou basest thing, avoid! hence, from my sight!
If after this command thou fraught the court
With thy unworthiness, thou diest: away!
Thou'rt poison to my blood.

POSTHUMUS LEONATUS: The gods protect you!
And bless the good remainders of the court! I am gone.

Exit

IMOGEN: There cannot be a pinch in death
More sharp than this is.

CYMBELINE: O disloyal thing,
That shouldst repair my youth, thou heap'st
A year's age on me.

IMOGEN: I beseech you, sir,
Harm not yourself with your vexation
I am senseless of your wrath; a touch more rare
Subdues all pangs, all fears.

CYMBELINE: Past grace? obedience?

IMOGEN: Past hope, and in despair; that way, past grace.

CYMBELINE: That mightst have had the sole son of my queen!

IMOGEN: O blest, that I might not! I chose an eagle,
And did avoid a puttock.

CYMBELINE: Thou took'st a beggar; wouldst have made my throne A seat for baseness.

IMOGEN: No; I rather added A lustre to it.

CYMBELINE: O thou vile one!

IMOGEN: Sir, It is your fault that I have loved Posthumus:
You bred him as my playfellow, and he is
A man worth any woman, overbuys me
Almost the sum he pays.

CYMBELINE: What, art thou mad?

IMOGEN: Almost, sir: heaven restore me! Would I were
A neat-herd's daughter, and my Leonatus
Our neighbour shepherd's son!

CYMBELINE: Thou foolish thing!

Re-enter QUEEN

They were again together: you have done
Not after our command. Away with her,
And pen her up.

QUEEN: Beseech your patience. Peace,
Dear lady daughter, peace! Sweet sovereign,
Leave us to ourselves; and make yourself some comfort
Out of your best advice.

CYMBELINE: Nay, let her languish
A drop of blood a day; and, being aged,
Die of this folly!

Exeunt CYMBELINE and Lords

QUEEN: Fie! you must give way.

Enter PISANIO

Here is your servant. How now, sir! What news?

PISANIO: My lord your son drew on my master.

QUEEN: Ha! No harm, I trust, is done?

PISANIO: There might have been,
But that my master rather play'd than fought
And had no help of anger: they were parted
By gentlemen at hand.

QUEEN: I am very glad on't.

IMOGEN: Your son's my father's friend; he takes his part.
To draw upon an exile! O brave sir!
I would they were in Afric both together;
Myself by with a needle, that I might prick
The goer-back. Why came you from your master?

PISANIO: On his command: he would not suffer me
To bring him to the haven; left these notes
Of what commands I should be subject to,
When 't pleased you to employ me.

QUEEN: This hath been Your faithful servant:
I dare lay mine honour He will remain so.

PISANIO: I humbly thank your highness.

QUEEN: Pray, walk awhile.

IMOGEN: About some half-hour hence,
I pray you, speak with me: you shall at least
Go see my lord aboard: for this time leave me.

Exeunt

SCENE II. The same. A public place.

Enter CLOTEN and two Lords

First Lord: Sir, I would advise you to shift a shirt; the
violence of action hath made you reek as a
sacrifice: where air comes out, air comes in:
there's none abroad so wholesome as that you vent.

CLOTEN: If my shirt were bloody, then to shift it. Have I hurt him?

Second Lord: *[Aside]* No, 'faith; not so much as his patience.

First Lord: Hurt him! his body's a passable carcass, if he be not hurt: it is a thoroughfare for steel, if it be not hurt.

Second Lord: *[Aside]* His steel was in debt; it went o' the backside the town.

CLOTEN: The villain would not stand me.

Second Lord: *[Aside]* No; but he fled forward still, toward your face.

First Lord: Stand you! You have land enough of your own: but he added to your having; gave you some ground.

Second Lord: *[Aside]* As many inches as you have oceans. Puppies!

CLOTEN: I would they had not come between us.

Second Lord: *[Aside]* So would I, till you had measured how long a fool you were upon the ground.

CLOTEN: And that she should love this fellow and refuse me!

Second Lord: *[Aside]* If it be a sin to make a true election, she is damned.

First Lord: Sir, as I told you always, her beauty and her brain go not together: she's a good sign, but I have seen small reflection of her wit.

Second Lord: *[Aside]* She shines not upon fools, lest the reflection should hurt her.

CLOTEN: Come, I'll to my chamber. Would there had been some hurt done!

Second Lord: *[Aside]* I wish not so; unless it had been the fall of an ass, which is no great hurt.

CLOTEN: You'll go with us?

First Lord: I'll attend your lordship.

CLOTEN: Nay, come, let's go together.

Second Lord: Well, my lord.

Exeunt

SCENE III. A room in Cymbeline's palace.

Enter IMOGEN and PISANIO

IMOGEN: I would thou grew'st unto the shores o' the haven,
And question'dst every sail: if he should write
And not have it, 'twere a paper lost,
As offer'd mercy is. What was the last
That he spake to thee?

PISANIO: It was his queen, his queen!

IMOGEN: Then waved his handkerchief?

PISANIO: And kiss'd it, madam.

IMOGEN: Senseless Linen! happier therein than I!
And that was all?

PISANIO: No, madam; for so long
As he could make me with this eye or ear
Distinguish him from others, he did keep
The deck, with glove, or hat, or handkerchief,
Still waving, as the fits and stirs of 's mind
Could best express how slow his soul sail'd on,
How swift his ship.

IMOGEN: Thou shouldst have made him
As little as a crow, or less, ere left
To after-eye him.

PISANIO: Madam, so I did.

IMOGEN: I would have broke mine eye-strings; crack'd them, but To look upon him, till the diminution Of space had pointed him sharp as my needle,
Nay, follow'd him, till he had melted from
The smallness of a gnat to air, and then
Have turn'd mine eye and wept. But, good PISANIO ,
When shall we hear from him?

PISANIO: Be assured, madam, With his next vantage.

IMOGEN: I did not take my leave of him, but had
Most pretty things to say: ere I could tell him
How I would think on him at certain hours
Such thoughts and such, or I could make him swear
The shes of Italy should not betray
Mine interest and his honour, or have charged him,
At the sixth hour of morn, at noon, at midnight,
To encounter me with orisons, for then
I am in heaven for him; or ere I could
Give him that parting kiss which I had set
Betwixt two charming words, comes in my father
And like the tyrannous breathing of the north
Shakes all our buds from growing.

Enter a Lady

Lady: The queen, madam, Desires your highness' company.

IMOGEN: Those things I bid you do, get them dispatch'd.
I will attend the queen.

PISANIO: Madam, I shall.

Exeunt

SCENE IV. Rome. Philario's house.

Enter PHILARIO, IACHIMO, a Frenchman, a Dutchman, and a Spaniard

IACHIMO: Believe it, sir, I have seen him in Britain: he was then of a crescent note, expected to prove so worthy as since he hath been allowed the name of; but I could then have looked on him without the help of admiration, though the catalogue of his endowments had been tabled by his side and I to peruse him by items.

PHILARIO: You speak of him when he was less furnished than now he is with that which makes him both without and within.

Frenchman: I have seen him in France: we had very many there could behold the sun with as firm eyes as he.

IACHIMO: This matter of marrying his king's daughter, wherein he must be weighed rather by her value than his own, words him, I doubt not, a great deal from the matter.

Frenchman: And then his banishment.

IACHIMO: Ay, and the approbation of those that weep this lamentable divorce under her colours are wonderfully to extend him; be it but to fortify her judgment, which else an easy battery might lay flat, for taking a beggar without less quality. But how comes

it he is to sojourn with you? How creeps
acquaintance?

PHILARIO: His father and I were soldiers together; to whom I have been often bound for no less than my life.
Here comes the Briton: let him be so entertained amongst you as suits, with gentlemen of your knowing, to a stranger of his quality.

Enter POSTHUMUS LEONATUS

I beseech you all, be better known to this gentleman; whom I commend to you as a noble friend of mine: how worthy he is I will leave to appear hereafter, rather than story him in his own hearing.

Frenchman: Sir, we have known together in Orleans.

POSTHUMUS LEONATUS: Since when I have been debtor to you for courtesies, which I will be ever to pay and yet pay still.

Frenchman: Sir, you o'er-rate my poor kindness: I was glad I did atone my countryman and you; it had been pity you should have been put together with so mortal a purpose as then each bore, upon importance of so slight and trivial a nature.

POSTHUMUS LEONATUS: By your pardon, sir, I was then a young traveller; rather shunned to go even with what I heard

than in my every action to be guided by others' experiences:
but upon my mended judgment--if I offend not to say
it is mended--my quarrel was not altogether slight.

Frenchman: 'Faith, yes, to be put to the arbitrement of swords,
and by such two that would by all likelihood have
confounded one the other, or have fallen both.

IACHIMO: Can we, with manners, ask what was the
difference?

Frenchman: Safely, I think: 'twas a contention in public,
which may, without contradiction, suffer the report.
It was much like an argument that fell out last
night, where each of us fell in praise of our
country mistresses; this gentleman at that time
vouching--and upon warrant of bloody
affirmation--his to be more fair, virtuous, wise,
chaste, constant-qualified and less attemptable
than any the rarest of our ladies in France.

IACHIMO: That lady is not now living, or this gentleman's
opinion by this worn out.

POSTHUMUS LEONATUS: She holds her virtue still and I my
mind.

IACHIMO: You must not so far prefer her 'fore ours of Italy.

POSTHUMUS LEONATUS: Being so far provoked as I was in France, I would abate her nothing, though I profess myself her adorer, not her friend.

IACHIMO: As fair and as good--a kind of hand-in-hand comparison--had been something too fair and too good for any lady in Britain. If she went before others I have seen, as that diamond of yours outlustres many I have beheld. I could not but believe she excelled many: but I have not seen the most precious diamond that is, nor you the lady.

POSTHUMUS LEONATUS: I praised her as I rated her: so do I my stone.

IACHIMO: What do you esteem it at?

POSTHUMUS LEONATUS: More than the world enjoys.

IACHIMO: Either your unparagoned mistress is dead, or she's outprized by a trifle.

POSTHUMUS LEONATUS: You are mistaken: the one may be sold, or given, if there were wealth enough for the purchase, or merit for the gift: the other is not a thing for sale, and only the gift of the gods.

IACHIMO: Which the gods have given you?

POSTHUMUS LEONATUS: Which, by their graces, I will keep.

IACHIMO: You may wear her in title yours: but, you know, strange fowl light upon neighbouring ponds. Your ring may be stolen too: so your brace of unprizable estimations; the one is but frail and the other casual; a cunning thief, or a that way accomplished courtier, would hazard the winning both of first and last.

POSTHUMUS LEONATUS: Your Italy contains none so accomplished a courtier to convince the honour of my mistress, if, in the holding or loss of that, you term her frail. I do nothing doubt you have store of thieves; notwithstanding, I fear not my ring.

PHILARIO: Let us leave here, gentlemen.

POSTHUMUS LEONATUS: Sir, with all my heart. This worthy signior, I thank him, makes no stranger of me; we are familiar at first.

IACHIMO: With five times so much conversation, I should get ground of your fair mistress, make her go back, even to the yielding, had I admittance and opportunity to friend.

POSTHUMUS LEONATUS: No, no.

IACHIMO: I dare thereupon pawn the moiety of my estate to your ring; which, in my opinion, o'ervalues it something: but I make my wager rather against your confidence than her reputation: and, to bar your offence herein too, I durst attempt it against any lady in the world.

POSTHUMUS LEONATUS: You are a great deal abused in too bold a persuasion; and I doubt not you sustain what you're worthy of by your attempt.

IACHIMO: What's that?

POSTHUMUS LEONATUS: A repulse: though your attempt, as you call it, deserve more; a punishment too.

PHILARIO: Gentlemen, enough of this: it came in too suddenly; let it die as it was born, and, I pray you, be better acquainted.

IACHIMO: Would I had put my estate and my neighbour's on the approbation of what I have spoke!

POSTHUMUS LEONATUS: What lady would you choose to assail?

IACHIMO: Yours; whom in constancy you think stands so safe. I will lay you ten thousand ducats to your ring, that, commend me to the court where your lady is, with no more advantage than the opportunity of a second conference, and I will bring from thence that honour of hers which you imagine so reserved.

POSTHUMUS LEONATUS: I will wage against your gold, gold to it: my ring I hold dear as my finger; 'tis part of it.

IACHIMO: You are afraid, and therein the wiser. If you buy ladies' flesh at a million a dram, you cannot preserve it from tainting: but I see you have some religion in you, that you fear.

POSTHUMUS LEONATUS: This is but a custom in your tongue; you bear a graver purpose, I hope.

IACHIMO: I am the master of my speeches, and would undergo what's spoken, I swear.

POSTHUMUS LEONATUS: Will you? I shall but lend my diamond till your return: let there be covenants drawn between's: my mistress exceeds in goodness the hugeness of your unworthy thinking: I dare you to this match: here's my ring.

PHILARIO: I will have it no lay.

IACHIMO: By the gods, it is one. If I bring you no sufficient testimony that I have enjoyed the dearest bodily part of your mistress, my ten thousand ducats are yours; so is your diamond too: if I come off, and leave her in such honour as you have trust in, she your jewel, this your jewel, and my gold are yours: provided I have your commendation for my more free entertainment.

POSTHUMUS LEONATUS: I embrace these conditions; let us have articles betwixt us. Only, thus far you shall answer: if you make your voyage upon her and give me directly to understand you have prevailed, I am no further your enemy; she is not worth our debate: if she remain unseduced, you not making it appear otherwise, for your ill opinion and the assault you have made to her chastity you shall answer me with your sword.

IACHIMO: Your hand; a covenant: we will have these things set down by lawful counsel, and straight away for Britain, lest the bargain should catch cold and starve: I will fetch my gold and have our two wagers recorded.

POSTHUMUS LEONATUS: Agreed.

Exeunt POSTHUMUS LEONATUS and IACHIMO

Frenchman: Will this hold, think you?

PHILARIO: Signior Iachimo will not from it.
Pray, let us follow 'em.

Exeunt

SCENE V. Britain. A room in Cymbeline's palace.

Enter QUEEN, Ladies, and CORNELIUS

QUEEN: Whiles yet the dew's on ground, gather those flowers; Make haste: who has the note of them?

First Lady: I, madam.

QUEEN: Dispatch.

Exeunt Ladies

Now, master doctor, have you brought those drugs?

CORNELIUS: Pleaseth your highness, ay: here they are, madam:

Presenting a small box

But I beseech your grace, without offence,--
My conscience bids me ask--wherefore you have
Commanded of me those most poisonous compounds,
Which are the movers of a languishing death;
But though slow, deadly?

QUEEN: I wonder, doctor, Thou ask'st me such a question.
Have I not been Thy pupil long? Hast thou not learn'd me how
To make perfumes? distil? preserve? yea, so
That our great king himself doth woo me oft

For my confections? Having thus far proceeded,--
Unless thou think'st me devilish--is't not meet
That I did amplify my judgment in
Other conclusions? I will try the forces
Of these thy compounds on such creatures as
We count not worth the hanging, but none human,
To try the vigour of them and apply
Allayments to their act, and by them gather
Their several virtues and effects.

CORNELIUS: Your highness
Shall from this practise but make hard your heart:
Besides, the seeing these effects will be
Both noisome and infectious.

QUEEN: O, content thee.

Enter PISANIO

Aside

Here comes a flattering rascal; upon him
Will I first work: he's for his master,
An enemy to my son. How now, PISANIO!
Doctor, your service for this time is ended;
Take your own way.

CORNELIUS: *[Aside]* I do suspect you, madam;
But you shall do no harm.

QUEEN: *[To PISANIO]* Hark thee, a word.

CORNELIUS: *[Aside]* I do not like her. She doth think she has
Strange lingering poisons: I do know her spirit,
And will not trust one of her malice with
A drug of such damn'd nature. Those she has
Will stupefy and dull the sense awhile;
Which first, perchance, she'll prove on
cats and dogs, Then afterward up higher: but there is
No danger in what show of death it makes,
More than the locking-up the spirits a time,
To be more fresh, reviving. She is fool'd
With a most false effect; and I the truer,
So to be false with her.

QUEEN: No further service, doctor,
Until I send for thee.

CORNELIUS: I humbly take my leave.

Exit

QUEEN: Weeps she still, say'st thou? Dost thou think in time
She will not quench and let instructions enter
Where folly now possesses? Do thou work:
When thou shalt bring me word she loves my son,
I'll tell thee on the instant thou art then
As great as is thy master, greater, for
His fortunes all lie speechless and his name
Is at last gasp: return he cannot, nor

Continue where he is: to shift his being
Is to exchange one misery with another,
And every day that comes comes to decay
A day's work in him. What shalt thou expect,
To be depender on a thing that leans,
Who cannot be new built, nor has no friends,
So much as but to prop him?

The QUEEN drops the box:
PISANIO takes it up

Thou takest up
Thou know'st not what; but take it for thy labour:
It is a thing I made, which hath the king
Five times redeem'd from death: I do not know
What is more cordial. Nay, I prethee, take it;
It is an earnest of a further good
That I mean to thee. Tell thy mistress how
The case stands with her; do't as from thyself.
Think what a chance thou changest on, but think
Thou hast thy mistress still, to boot, my son,
Who shall take notice of thee: I'll move the king
To any shape of thy preferment such
As thou'lt desire; and then myself, I chiefly,
That set thee on to this desert, am bound
To load thy merit richly. Call my women:
Think on my words.

Exit

PISANIO: A sly and constant knave,
Not to be shaked; the agent for his master
And the remembrancer of her to hold
The hand-fast to her lord. I have given him that
Which, if he take, shall quite unpeople her
Of liegers for her sweet, and which she after,
Except she bend her humour, shall be assured
To taste of too.

Re-enter PISANIO and Ladies

So, so: well done, well done:
The violets, cowslips, and the primroses,
Bear to my closet. Fare thee well,
PISANIO; Think on my words.

Exeunt QUEEN and Ladies

PISANIO: And shall do: But when to my good lord I prove untrue, I'll choke myself: there's all I'll do for you.

Exit

SCENE VI. The same. Another room in the palace.

Enter IMOGEN

IMOGEN: A father cruel, and a step-dame false;
A foolish suitor to a wedded lady,

That hath her husband banish'd;--O, that husband!
My supreme crown of grief! and those repeated
Vexations of it! Had I been thief-stol'n,
As my two brothers, happy! but most miserable
Is the desire that's glorious: blest be those,
How mean soe'er, that have their honest wills,
Which seasons comfort. Who may this be? Fie!

Enter PISANIO and IACHIMO

PISANIO: Madam, a noble gentleman of Rome,
Comes from my lord with letters.

IACHIMO: Change you, madam?
The worthy Leonatus is in safety
And greets your highness dearly.

Presents a letter

IMOGEN: Thanks, good sir: You're kindly welcome.

IACHIMO: *[Aside]* All of her that is out of door most rich!
If she be furnish'd with a mind so rare,
She is alone the Arabian bird, and I
Have lost the wager. Boldness be my friend!
Arm me, audacity, from head to foot!
Or, like the Parthian, I shall flying fight;
Rather directly fly.

IMOGEN: [Reads] 'He is one of the noblest note, to whose

kindnesses I am most infinitely tied. Reflect upon
him accordingly, as you value your trust--
LEONATUS.' So far I read aloud:
But even the very middle of my heart
Is warm'd by the rest, and takes it thankfully.
You are as welcome, worthy sir, as I
Have words to bid you, and shall find it so
In all that I can do.

IACHIMO: Thanks, fairest lady.
What, are men mad? Hath nature given them eyes
To see this vaulted arch, and the rich crop
Of sea and land, which can distinguish 'twixt
The fiery orbs above and the twinn'd stones
Upon the number'd beach? and can we not
Partition make with spectacles so precious
'Twixt fair and foul?

IMOGEN: What makes your admiration?

IACHIMO: It cannot be i' the eye, for apes and monkeys
'Twixt two such shes would chatter this way and
Contemn with mows the other; nor i' the judgment,
For idiots in this case of favour would
Be wisely definite; nor i' the appetite;
Sluttery to such neat excellence opposed
Should make desire vomit emptiness,
Not so allured to feed.

IMOGEN: What is the matter, trow?

IACHIMO: The cloyed will,
That satiate yet unsatisfied desire, that tub
Both fill'd and running, ravening first the lamb
Longs after for the garbage.

IMOGEN: What, dear sir,
Thus raps you? Are you well?

IACHIMO: Thanks, madam; well.
To PISANIO: Beseech you, sir, desire
My man's abode where I did leave him: he
Is strange and peevish.

PISANIO: I was going, sir,
To give him welcome.

Exit

IMOGEN: Continues well my lord? His health, beseech you?

IACHIMO: Well, madam.

IMOGEN: Is he disposed to mirth? I hope he is.

IACHIMO: Exceeding pleasant; none a stranger there
So merry and so gamesome: he is call'd
The Briton reveller.

IMOGEN: When he was here,

He did incline to sadness, and oft-times
Not knowing why.

IACHIMO: I never saw him sad.
There is a Frenchman his companion, one
An eminent monsieur, that, it seems, much loves
A Gallian girl at home; he furnaces
The thick sighs from him, whiles the jolly Briton--
Your lord, I mean--laughs from's free lungs, cries 'O,
Can my sides hold, to think that man, who knows
By history, report, or his own proof,
What woman is, yea, what she cannot choose
But must be, will his free hours languish for
Assured bondage?'

IMOGEN: Will my lord say so?

IACHIMO: Ay, madam, with his eyes in flood with laughter:
It is a recreation to be by And hear him mock the Frenchman.
But, heavens know, Some men are much to blame.

IMOGEN: Not he, I hope.

IACHIMO: Not he: but yet heaven's bounty towards him might
Be used more thankfully. In himself, 'tis much;
In you, which I account his beyond all talents,
Whilst I am bound to wonder, I am bound
To pity too.

IMOGEN: What do you pity, sir?

IACHIMO: Two creatures heartily.

IMOGEN: Am I one, sir? You look on me: what wreck discern you in me Deserves your pity?

IACHIMO: Lamentable! What, To hide me from the radiant sun and solace I' the dungeon by a snuff?

IMOGEN: I pray you, sir,
Deliver with more openness your answers
To my demands. Why do you pity me?

IACHIMO: That others do--
I was about to say--enjoy your--But
It is an office of the gods to venge it,
Not mine to speak on 't.

IMOGEN: You do seem to know
Something of me, or what concerns me: pray you,--
Since doubling things go ill often hurts more
Than to be sure they do; for certainties
Either are past remedies, or, timely knowing,
The remedy then born--discover to me
What both you spur and stop.

IACHIMO: Had I this cheek
To bathe my lips upon; this hand, whose touch,
Whose every touch, would force the feeler's soul
To the oath of loyalty; this object, which

Takes prisoner the wild motion of mine eye,
Fixing it only here; should I, damn'd then,
Slaver with lips as common as the stairs
That mount the Capitol; join gripes with hands
Made hard with hourly falsehood--falsehood, as
With labour; then by-peeping in an eye
Base and unlustrous as the smoky light
That's fed with stinking tallow; it were fit
That all the plagues of hell should at one time
Encounter such revolt.

IMOGEN: My lord, I fear, Has forgot Britain.

IACHIMO: And himself. Not I,
Inclined to this intelligence, pronounce
The beggary of his change; but 'tis your graces
That from pay mutest conscience to my tongue
Charms this report out.

IMOGEN: Let me hear no more.

IACHIMO: O dearest soul! your cause doth strike my heart
With pity, that doth make me sick. A lady
So fair, and fasten'd to an empery,
Would make the great'st king double,--to be partner'd
With tomboys hired with that self-exhibition
Which your own coffers yield! with diseased ventures
That play with all infirmities for gold
Which rottenness can lend nature! such boil'd stuff
As well might poison poison! Be revenged;

Or she that bore you was no queen, and you
Recoil from your great stock.

IMOGEN: Revenged!
How should I be revenged? If this be true,--
As I have such a heart that both mine ears
Must not in haste abuse--if it be true,
How should I be revenged?

IACHIMO: Should he make me
Live, like Diana's priest, betwixt cold sheets,
Whiles he is vaulting variable ramps,
In your despite, upon your purse? Revenge it.
I dedicate myself to your sweet pleasure,
More noble than that runagate to your bed,
And will continue fast to your affection,
Still close as sure.

IMOGEN: What, ho, PISANIO!

IACHIMO: Let me my service tender on your lips.

IMOGEN: Away! I do condemn mine ears that have
So long attended thee. If thou wert honourable,
Thou wouldst have told this tale for virtue, not
For such an end thou seek'st,--as base as strange.
Thou wrong'st a gentleman, who is as far
From thy report as thou from honour, and
Solicit'st here a lady that disdains
Thee and the devil alike. What ho,

PISANIO! The king my father shall be made acquainted
Of thy assault: if he shall think it fit,
A saucy stranger in his court to mart
As in a Romish stew and to expound
His beastly mind to us, he hath a court
He little cares for and a daughter who
He not respects at all. What, ho, PISANIO!

IACHIMO: O happy Leonatus! I may say
The credit that thy lady hath of thee
Deserves thy trust, and thy most perfect goodness
Her assured credit. Blessed live you long!
A lady to the worthiest sir that ever
Country call'd his! and you his mistress, only
For the most worthiest fit! Give me your pardon.
I have spoke this, to know if your affiance
Were deeply rooted; and shall make your lord,
That which he is, new o'er: and he is one
The truest manner'd; such a holy witch
That he enchants societies into him;
Half all men's hearts are his.

IMOGEN: You make amends.

IACHIMO: He sits 'mongst men like a descended god:
He hath a kind of honour sets him off,
More than a mortal seeming. Be not angry,
Most mighty princess, that I have adventured
To try your taking a false report; which hath
Honour'd with confirmation your great judgment

In the election of a sir so rare,
Which you know cannot err: the love I bear him
Made me to fan you thus, but the gods made you,
Unlike all others, chaffless. Pray, your pardon.

IMOGEN: All's well, sir: take my power i' the court
for yours.

IACHIMO: My humble thanks. I had almost forgot
To entreat your grace but in a small request,
And yet of moment to, for it concerns
Your lord; myself and other noble friends,
Are partners in the business.

IMOGEN: Pray, what is't?

IACHIMO: Some dozen Romans of us and your lord--
The best feather of our wing--have mingled sums
To buy a present for the emperor
Which I, the factor for the rest, have done
In France: 'tis plate of rare device, and jewels
Of rich and exquisite form; their values great;
And I am something curious, being strange,
To have them in safe stowage: may it please you
To take them in protection?

IMOGEN: Willingly; And pawn mine honour for their safety:
since My lord hath interest in them, I will keep them
In my bedchamber.

IACHIMO: They are in a trunk,
Attended by my men: I will make bold
To send them to you, only for this night;
I must aboard to-morrow.

IMOGEN: O, no, no.

IACHIMO: Yes, I beseech; or I shall short my word
By lengthening my return. From Gallia
I cross'd the seas on purpose and on promise
To see your grace.

IMOGEN: I thank you for your pains:
But not away to-morrow!

IACHIMO: O, I must, madam:
Therefore I shall beseech you, if you please
To greet your lord with writing, do't to-night:
I have outstood my time; which is material
To the tender of our present.

IMOGEN: I will write. Send your trunk to me; it shall safe be kept, And truly yielded you. You're very welcome.

Exeunt

ACT II. SCENE I. Britain. Before Cymbeline's palace.

Enter CLOTEN and two Lords

CLOTEN: Was there ever man had such luck! when I kissed the jack, upon an up-cast to be hit away! I had a hundred pound on't: and then a whoreson jackanapes must take me up for swearing; as if I borrowed mine oaths of him and might not spend them at my pleasure.

First Lord: What got he by that? You have broke his pate with your bowl.

Second Lord: *[Aside]* If his wit had been like him that broke it, it would have run all out.

CLOTEN: When a gentleman is disposed to swear, it is not for any standers-by to curtail his oaths, ha?

Second Lord: No my lord;

[Aside] nor crop the ears of them.

CLOTEN: Whoreson dog! I give him satisfaction? Would he had been one of my rank!

Second Lord: *[Aside]* To have smelt like a fool.

CLOTEN: I am not vexed more at any thing in the earth: a pox on't! I had rather not be so noble as I am; they dare not fight with me, because of the queen my mother: every Jack-slave hath his bellyful of fighting, and I must go up and down like a cock that nobody can match.

Second Lord: *[Aside]* You are cock and capon too; and you crow, cock, with your comb on.

CLOTEN: Sayest thou?

Second Lord: It is not fit your lordship should undertake every companion that you give offence to.

CLOTEN: No, I know that: but it is fit I should commit offence to my inferiors.

Second Lord: Ay, it is fit for your lordship only.

CLOTEN: Why, so I say.

First Lord: Did you hear of a stranger that's come to court to-night?

CLOTEN: A stranger, and I not know on't!

Second Lord: *[Aside]* He's a strange fellow himself, and knows it not.

First Lord: There's an Italian come; and, 'tis thought, one of Leonatus' friends.

CLOTEN: Leonatus! a banished rascal; and he's another, whatsoever he be. Who told you of this stranger?

First Lord: One of your lordship's pages.

CLOTEN: Is it fit I went to look upon him? is there no derogation in't?

Second Lord: You cannot derogate, my lord.

CLOTEN: Not easily, I think.

Second Lord: *[Aside]* You are a fool granted; therefore your issues, being foolish, do not derogate.

CLOTEN: Come, I'll go see this Italian: what I have lost to-day at bowls I'll win to-night of him. Come, go.

Second Lord: I'll attend your lordship.

Exeunt CLOTEN and First Lord:

That such a crafty devil as is his mother Should yield the world this ass! a woman that
Bears all down with her brain; and this her son
Cannot take two from twenty, for his heart,
And leave eighteen. Alas, poor princess,
Thou divine Imogen, what thou endurest,
Betwixt a father by thy step-dame govern'd,
A mother hourly coining plots, a wooer
More hateful than the foul expulsion is
Of thy dear husband, than that horrid act

Of the divorce he'ld make! The heavens hold firm
The walls of thy dear honour, keep unshaked
That temple, thy fair mind, that thou mayst stand,
To enjoy thy banish'd lord and this great land!

Exit

SCENE II. Imogen's bedchamber in Cymbeline's palace: a trunk in one corner of it.

IMOGEN in bed, reading; a Lady attending

IMOGEN: Who's there? my woman Helen?

Lady: Please you, madam

IMOGEN: What hour is it?

Lady: Almost midnight, madam.

IMOGEN: I have read three hours then: mine eyes are weak:
Fold down the leaf where I have left: to bed:
Take not away the taper, leave it burning;
And if thou canst awake by four o' the clock,
I prithee, call me. Sleep hath seized me wholly

Exit Lady

To your protection I commend me, gods.

From fairies and the tempters of the night
Guard me, beseech ye.

Sleeps. IACHIMO comes from the trunk

IACHIMO: The crickets sing, and man's o'er-labour'd sense
Repairs itself by rest. Our Tarquin thus
Did softly press the rushes, ere he waken'd
The chastity he wounded. Cytherea,
How bravely thou becomest thy bed, fresh lily,
And whiter than the sheets! That I might touch!
But kiss; one kiss! Rubies unparagon'd,
How dearly they do't! 'Tis her breathing that
Perfumes the chamber thus: the flame o' the taper
Bows toward her, and would under-peep her lids,
To see the enclosed lights, now canopied
Under these windows, white and azure laced
With blue of heaven's own tinct. But my design,
To note the chamber: I will write all down:
Such and such pictures; there the window; such
The adornment of her bed; the arras; figures,
Why, such and such; and the contents o' the story.
Ah, but some natural notes about her body,
Above ten thousand meaner moveables
Would testify, to enrich mine inventory.
O sleep, thou ape of death, lie dull upon her!
And be her sense but as a monument,
Thus in a chapel lying! Come off, come off:

Taking off her bracelet

As slippery as the Gordian knot was hard!
'Tis mine; and this will witness outwardly,
As strongly as the conscience does within,
To the madding of her lord. On her left breast
A mole cinque-spotted, like the crimson drops
I' the bottom of a cowslip: here's a voucher,
Stronger than ever law could make: this secret
Will force him think I have pick'd the lock and ta'en
The treasure of her honour. No more. To what end?
Why should I write this down, that's riveted,
Screw'd to my memory? She hath been reading late
The tale of Tereus; here the leaf's turn'd down
Where Philomel gave up. I have enough:
To the trunk again, and shut the spring of it.
Swift, swift, you dragons of the night, that dawning
May bare the raven's eye! I lodge in fear;
Though this a heavenly angel, hell is here.

Clock strikes

One, two, three: time, time!

Goes into the trunk. The scene closes

Scene III. An ante-chamber adjoining Imogen's apartments.

Enter CLOTEN and Lords

First Lord: Your lordship is the most patient man in loss, the most coldest that ever turned up ace.

CLOTEN: It would make any man cold to lose.

First Lord: But not every man patient after the noble temper of your lordship. You are most hot and furious when you win.

CLOTEN: Winning will put any man into courage. If I could get this foolish Imogen, I should have gold enough.
It's almost morning, is't not?

First Lord: Day, my lord.

CLOTEN: I would this music would come: I am advised to give her music o' mornings; they say it will penetrate.

Enter Musicians

Come on; tune: if you can penetrate her with your
fingering, so; we'll try with tongue too: if none
will do, let her remain; but I'll never give o'er.
First, a very excellent good-conceited thing;
after, a wonderful sweet air, with admirable rich
words to it: and then let her consider.

SONG
Hark, hark! the lark at heaven's gate sings,
And Phoebus 'gins arise,

His steeds to water at those springs
On chaliced flowers that lies;
And winking Mary-buds begin
To ope their golden eyes:
With every thing that pretty is,
My lady sweet, arise:
Arise, arise.

CLOTEN: So, get you gone. If this penetrate, I will consider your music the better: if it do not, it is a vice in her ears, which horse-hairs and calves'-guts, nor the voice of unpaved eunuch to boot, can never amend.

Exeunt Musicians

Second Lord: Here comes the king.

CLOTEN: I am glad I was up so late; for that's the reason I was up so early: he cannot choose but take this service I have done fatherly.

Enter CYMBELINE and QUEEN

Good morrow to your majesty and to my gracious mother.

CYMBELINE: Attend you here the door of our stern daughter? Will she not forth?

CLOTEN: I have assailed her with music, but she vouchsafes no notice.

CYMBELINE: The exile of her minion is too new;
She hath not yet forgot him: some more time
Must wear the print of his remembrance out,
And then she's yours.

QUEEN: You are most bound to the king,
Who lets go by no vantages that may
Prefer you to his daughter. Frame yourself
To orderly soliciting, and be friended
With aptness of the season; make denials
Increase your services; so seem as if
You were inspired to do those duties which
You tender to her; that you in all obey her,
Save when command to your dismission tends,
And therein you are senseless.

CLOTEN: Senseless! not so.

Enter a Messenger

Messenger: So like you, sir, ambassadors from Rome;
The one is Caius Lucius.

CYMBELINE: A worthy fellow,
Albeit he comes on angry purpose now;
But that's no fault of his: we must receive him
According to the honour of his sender;

And towards himself, his goodness forespent on us,
We must extend our notice. Our dear son,
When you have given good morning to your mistress,
Attend the queen and us; we shall have need
To employ you towards this Roman. Come, our queen.

Exeunt all but CLOTEN

CLOTEN: If she be up, I'll speak with her; if not,
Let her lie still and dream.

Knocks

By your leave, ho!
I Know her women are about her: what
If I do line one of their hands? 'Tis gold
Which buys admittance; oft it doth; yea, and makes
Diana's rangers false themselves, yield up
Their deer to the stand o' the stealer; and 'tis gold
Which makes the true man kill'd and saves the thief;
Nay, sometime hangs both thief and true man: what
Can it not do and undo? I will make
One of her women lawyer to me, for
I yet not understand the case myself.

Knocks

By your leave.

Enter a Lady

Lady: Who's there that knocks?

CLOTEN: A gentleman.

Lady: No more?

CLOTEN: Yes, and a gentlewoman's son.

Lady: That's more Than some, whose tailors are as dear as yours, Can justly boast of. What's your lordship's pleasure?

CLOTEN: Your lady's person: is she ready?

Lady: Ay,To keep her chamber.

CLOTEN: There is gold for you; Sell me your good report.

Lady: How! my good name? or to report of you
What I shall think is good?--The princess!

Enter IMOGEN

CLOTEN: Good morrow, fairest: sister, your sweet hand.

Exit Lady

IMOGEN: Good morrow, sir. You lay out too much pains
For purchasing but trouble; the thanks I give
Is telling you that I am poor of thanks

And scarce can spare them.

CLOTEN: Still, I swear I love you.

IMOGEN: If you but said so, 'twere as deep with me:
If you swear still, your recompense is still
That I regard it not.

CLOTEN: This is no answer.

IMOGEN: But that you shall not say I yield being silent,
I would not speak. I pray you, spare me: 'faith,
I shall unfold equal discourtesy
To your best kindness: one of your great knowing
Should learn, being taught, forbearance.

CLOTEN: To leave you in your madness, 'twere my sin:
I will not.

IMOGEN: Fools are not mad folks.

CLOTEN: Do you call me fool?

IMOGEN: As I am mad, I do:
If you'll be patient, I'll no more be mad;
That cures us both. I am much sorry, sir,
You put me to forget a lady's manners,
By being so verbal: and learn now, for all,
That I, which know my heart, do here pronounce,
By the very truth of it, I care not for you,

And am so near the lack of charity--
To accuse myself--I hate you; which I had rather
You felt than make't my boast.

CLOTEN: You sin against
Obedience, which you owe your father. For
The contract you pretend with that base wretch,
One bred of alms and foster'd with cold dishes,
With scraps o' the court, it is no contract, none:
And though it be allow'd in meaner parties--
Yet who than he more mean?--to knit their souls,
On whom there is no more dependency
But brats and beggary, in self-figured knot;
Yet you are curb'd from that enlargement by
The consequence o' the crown, and must not soil
The precious note of it with a base slave.
A hilding for a livery, a squire's cloth,
A pantler, not so eminent.

IMOGEN: Profane fellow
Wert thou the son of Jupiter and no more
But what thou art besides, thou wert too base
To be his groom: thou wert dignified enough,
Even to the point of envy, if 'twere made
Comparative for your virtues, to be styled
The under-hangman of his kingdom, and hated
For being preferred so well.

CLOTEN: The south-fog rot him!

IMOGEN: He never can meet more mischance than come
To be but named of thee. His meanest garment,
That ever hath but clipp'd his body, is dearer
In my respect than all the hairs above thee,
Were they all made such men. How now, PISANIO !

Enter PISANIO

CLOTEN: 'His garment!' Now the devil--

IMOGEN: To Dorothy my woman hie thee presently--

CLOTEN: 'His garment!'

IMOGEN: I am sprited with a fool.
Frighted, and anger'd worse: go bid my woman
Search for a jewel that too casually
Hath left mine arm: it was thy master's: 'shrew me,
If I would lose it for a revenue
Of any king's in Europe. I do think
I saw't this morning: confident I am
Last night 'twas on mine arm; I kiss'd it:
I hope it be not gone to tell my lord
That I kiss aught but he.

PISANIO: 'Twill not be lost.

IMOGEN: I hope so: go and search.

Exit PISANIO

CLOTEN: You have abused me:
'His meanest garment!'

IMOGEN: Ay, I said so, sir:
If you will make't an action, call witness to't.

CLOTEN: I will inform your father.

IMOGEN: Your mother too:
She's my good lady, and will conceive, I hope,
But the worst of me. So, I leave you, sir,
To the worst of discontent.

Exit

CLOTEN: I'll be revenged: 'His meanest garment!' Well.

Exit CYMBELINE

SCENE IV. Rome. Philario's house.

Enter POSTHUMUS and PHILARIO

POSTHUMUS LEONATUS: Fear it not, sir: I would I were so sure To win the king as I am bold her honour
Will remain hers.

PHILARIO: What means do you make to him?

POSTHUMUS LEONATUS: Not any, but abide the change of time, Quake in the present winter's state and wish
That warmer days would come: in these sear'd hopes,
I barely gratify your love; they failing,
I must die much your debtor.

PHILARIO: Your very goodness and your company
O'erpays all I can do. By this, your king
Hath heard of great Augustus: Caius Lucius
Will do's commission throughly: and I think
He'll grant the tribute, send the arrearages,
Or look upon our Romans, whose remembrance
Is yet fresh in their grief.

POSTHUMUS LEONATUS: I do believe,
Statist though I am none, nor like to be,
That this will prove a war; and you shall hear
The legions now in Gallia sooner landed
In our not-fearing Britain than have tidings
Of any penny tribute paid. Our countrymen
Are men more order'd than when Julius Caesar
Smiled at their lack of skill, but found their courage
Worthy his frowning at: their discipline,
Now mingled with their courages, will make known
To their approvers they are people such
That mend upon the world.

Enter IACHIMO

PHILARIO: See! Iachimo!

POSTHUMUS LEONATUS: The swiftest harts have posted you by land; And winds of all the comers kiss'd your sails, To make your vessel nimble.

PHILARIO: Welcome, sir.

POSTHUMUS LEONATUS: I hope the briefness of your answer made The speediness of your return.

IACHIMO: Your lady Is one of the fairest that I have look'd upon.

POSTHUMUS LEONATUS: And therewithal the best; or let her beauty Look through a casement to allure false hearts And be false with them.

IACHIMO: Here are letters for you.

POSTHUMUS LEONATUS: Their tenor good, I trust.

IACHIMO: 'Tis very like.

PHILARIO: Was Caius Lucius in the Britain court
When you were there?

IACHIMO: He was expected then,
But not approach'd.

POSTHUMUS LEONATUS: All is well yet.
Sparkles this stone as it was wont? or is't not
Too dull for your good wearing?

IACHIMO: If I had lost it,
I should have lost the worth of it in gold.
I'll make a journey twice as far, to enjoy
A second night of such sweet shortness which
Was mine in Britain, for the ring is won.

POSTHUMUS LEONATUS: The stone's too hard to come by.

IACHIMO: Not a whit, Your lady being so easy.

POSTHUMUS LEONATUS: Make not, sir,
Your loss your sport: I hope you know that we
Must not continue friends.

IACHIMO: Good sir, we must,
If you keep covenant. Had I not brought
The knowledge of your mistress home, I grant
We were to question further: but I now
Profess myself the winner of her honour,
Together with your ring; and not the wronger
Of her or you, having proceeded but
By both your wills.

POSTHUMUS LEONATUS: If you can make't apparent
That you have tasted her in bed, my hand
And ring is yours; if not, the foul opinion

You had of her pure honour gains or loses
Your sword or mine, or masterless leaves both
To who shall find them.

IACHIMO: Sir, my circumstances,
Being so near the truth as I will make them,
Must first induce you to believe: whose strength
I will confirm with oath; which, I doubt not,
You'll give me leave to spare, when you shall find
You need it not.

POSTHUMUS LEONATUS: Proceed.

IACHIMO: First, her bedchamber,--
Where, I confess, I slept not, but profess
Had that was well worth watching--it was hang'd
With tapesty of silk and silver; the story
Proud Cleopatra, when she met her Roman,
And Cydnus swell'd above the banks, or for
The press of boats or pride: a piece of work
So bravely done, so rich, that it did strive
In workmanship and value; which I wonder'd
Could be so rarely and exactly wrought,
Since the true life on't was--

POSTHUMUS LEONATUS: This is true;
And this you might have heard of here, by me,
Or by some other.

IACHIMO: More particulars

Must justify my knowledge.

POSTHUMUS LEONATUS: So they must,
Or do your honour injury.

IACHIMO: The chimney
Is south the chamber, and the chimney-piece
Chaste Dian bathing: never saw I figures
So likely to report themselves: the cutter
Was as another nature, dumb; outwent her,
Motion and breath left out.

POSTHUMUS LEONATUS: This is a thing
Which you might from relation likewise reap,
Being, as it is, much spoke of.

IACHIMO: The roof o' the chamber
With golden cherubins is fretted: her andirons--
I had forgot them--were two winking Cupids
Of silver, each on one foot standing, nicely
Depending on their brands.

POSTHUMUS LEONATUS: This is her honour!
Let it be granted you have seen all this--and praise
Be given to your remembrance--the description
Of what is in her chamber nothing saves
The wager you have laid.

IACHIMO: Then, if you can,

Showing the bracelet

Be pale: I beg but leave to air this jewel; see!
And now 'tis up again: it must be married
To that your diamond; I'll keep them.

POSTHUMUS LEONATUS: Jove!
Once more let me behold it: is it that
Which I left with her?

IACHIMO: Sir--I thank her--that:
She stripp'd it from her arm; I see her yet;
Her pretty action did outsell her gift,
And yet enrich'd it too: she gave it me, and said
She prized it once.

POSTHUMUS LEONATUS: May be she pluck'd it off
To send it me.

IACHIMO: She writes so to you, doth she?

POSTHUMUS LEONATUS: O, no, no, no! 'tis true. Here, take this too;

Gives the ring

It is a basilisk unto mine eye,
Kills me to look on't. Let there be no honour
Where there is beauty; truth, where semblance; love,
Where there's another man: the vows of women

Of no more bondage be, to where they are made,
Than they are to their virtues; which is nothing.
O, above measure false!

PHILARIO: Have patience, sir,
And take your ring again; 'tis not yet won:
It may be probable she lost it; or
Who knows if one of her women, being corrupted,
Hath stol'n it from her?

POSTHUMUS LEONATUS: Very true;
And so, I hope, he came by't. Back my ring:
Render to me some corporal sign about her,
More evident than this; for this was stolen.

IACHIMO: By Jupiter, I had it from her arm.

POSTHUMUS LEONATUS: Hark you, he swears; by Jupiter
he swears. 'Tis true:--nay, keep the ring--'tis true: I am sure
She would not lose it: her attendants are
All sworn and honourable:--they induced to steal it!
And by a stranger!--No, he hath enjoyed her:
The cognizance of her incontinency
Is this: she hath bought the name of whore
thus dearly. There, take thy hire; and all the fiends of hell
Divide themselves between you!

PHILARIO: Sir, be patient:
This is not strong enough to be believed
Of one persuaded well of--

POSTHUMUS LEONATUS: Never talk on't;
She hath been colted by him.

IACHIMO: If you seek
For further satisfying, under her breast--
Worthy the pressing--lies a mole, right proud
Of that most delicate lodging: by my life,
I kiss'd it; and it gave me present hunger
To feed again, though full. You do remember
This stain upon her?

POSTHUMUS LEONATUS: Ay, and it doth confirm
Another stain, as big as hell can hold,
Were there no more but it.

IACHIMO: Will you hear more?

POSTHUMUS LEONATUS: Spare your arithmetic: never count the turns; Once, and a million!

IACHIMO: I'll be sworn--

POSTHUMUS LEONATUS: No swearing.
If you will swear you have not done't, you lie;
And I will kill thee, if thou dost deny
Thou'st made me cuckold.

IACHIMO: I'll deny nothing.

POSTHUMUS LEONATUS: O, that I had her here, to tear her limb-meal! I will go there and do't, i' the court, before
Her father. I'll do something—

Exit

PHILARIO: Quite besides
The government of patience! You have won:
Let's follow him, and pervert the present wrath
He hath against himself.

IACHIMO: With an my heart.

Exeunt

SCENE V. Another room in Philario's house.

Enter POSTHUMUS LEONATUS

POSTHUMUS LEONATUS: Is there no way for men to be but women Must be half-workers? We are all bastards;
And that most venerable man which I
Did call my father, was I know not where
When I was stamp'd; some coiner with his tools
Made me a counterfeit: yet my mother seem'd
The Dian of that time so doth my wife
The nonpareil of this. O, vengeance, vengeance!
Me of my lawful pleasure she restrain'd
And pray'd me oft forbearance; did it with

A pudency so rosy the sweet view on't
Might well have warm'd old Saturn; that I thought her
As chaste as unsunn'd snow. O, all the devils!
This yellow Iachimo, in an hour,--wast not?--
Or less,--at first?--perchance he spoke not, but,
Like a full-acorn'd boar, a German one,
Cried 'O!' and mounted; found no opposition
But what he look'd for should oppose and she
Should from encounter guard. Could I find out
The woman's part in me! For there's no motion
That tends to vice in man, but I affirm
It is the woman's part: be it lying, note it,
The woman's; flattering, hers; deceiving, hers;
Lust and rank thoughts, hers, hers; revenges, hers;
Ambitions, covetings, change of prides, disdain,
Nice longing, slanders, mutability,
All faults that may be named, nay, that hell knows,
Why, hers, in part or all; but rather, all;
For even to vice
They are not constant but are changing still
One vice, but of a minute old, for one
Not half so old as that. I'll write against them,
Detest them, curse them: yet 'tis greater skill
In a true hate, to pray they have their will:
The very devils cannot plague them better.

Exit

ACT III. SCENE I. Britain. A hall in Cymbeline's palace.

Enter in state, CYMBELINE, QUEEN, CLOTEN, and Lords at one door, and at another, CAIUS LUCIUS and Attendants

CYMBELINE: Now say, what would Augustus Caesar with us?

CAIUS LUCIUS: When Julius Caesar, whose remembrance yet Lives in men's eyes and will to ears and tongues
Be theme and hearing ever, was in this Britain
And conquer'd it, Cassibelan, thine uncle,--
Famous in Caesar's praises, no whit less
Than in his feats deserving it--for him
And his succession granted Rome a tribute,
Yearly three thousand pounds, which by thee lately
Is left untender'd.

QUEEN: And, to kill the marvel, Shall be so ever.

CLOTEN: There be many Caesars,
Ere such another Julius. Britain is
A world by itself; and we will nothing pay
For wearing our own noses.

QUEEN: That opportunity
Which then they had to take from 's, to resume
We have again. Remember, sir, my liege,
The kings your ancestors, together with
The natural bravery of your isle, which stands
As Neptune's park, ribbed and paled in

With rocks unscalable and roaring waters,
With sands that will not bear your enemies' boats,
But suck them up to the topmast. A kind of conquest
Caesar made here; but made not here his brag
Of 'Came' and 'saw' and 'overcame: ' with shame--
That first that ever touch'd him--he was carried
From off our coast, twice beaten; and his shipping--
Poor ignorant baubles!-- upon our terrible seas,
Like egg-shells moved upon their surges, crack'd
As easily 'gainst our rocks: for joy whereof
The famed Cassibelan, who was once at point--
O giglot fortune!--to master Caesar's sword,
Made Lud's town with rejoicing fires bright
And Britons strut with courage.

CLOTEN: Come, there's no more tribute to be paid: our
kingdom is stronger than it was at that time; and,
as I said, there is no moe such Caesars: other of
them may have crook'd noses, but to owe such
straight arms, none.

CYMBELINE: Son, let your mother end.

CLOTEN: We have yet many among us can gripe as hard as
Cassibelan: I do not say I am one; but I have a
hand. Why tribute? why should we pay tribute? If
Caesar can hide the sun from us with a blanket, or
put the moon in his pocket, we will pay him tribute
for light; else, sir, no more tribute, pray you now.

CYMBELINE: You must know,
Till the injurious Romans did extort
This tribute from us, we were free:
Caesar's ambition,
Which swell'd so much that it did almost stretch
The sides o' the world, against all colour here
Did put the yoke upon 's; which to shake off
Becomes a warlike people, whom we reckon
Ourselves to be.

CLOTEN: Lords We do.

CYMBELINE: Say, then, to Caesar,
Our ancestor was that Mulmutius which
Ordain'd our laws, whose use the sword of Caesar
Hath too much mangled; whose repair and franchise
Shall, by the power we hold, be our good deed,
Though Rome be therefore angry: Mulmutius made our laws,
Who was the first of Britain which did put
His brows within a golden crown and call'd
Himself a king.

CAIUS LUCIUS: I am sorry, Cymbeline,
That I am to pronounce Augustus Caesar--
Caesar, that hath more kings his servants than
Thyself domestic officers--thine enemy:
Receive it from me, then: war and confusion
In Caesar's name pronounce I 'gainst thee: look
For fury not to be resisted. Thus defied,
I thank thee for myself.

CYMBELINE: Thou art welcome, Caius.
Thy Caesar knighted me; my youth I spent
Much under him; of him I gather'd honour;
Which he to seek of me again, perforce,
Behoves me keep at utterance. I am perfect
That the Pannonians and Dalmatians for
Their liberties are now in arms; a precedent
Which not to read would show the Britons cold:
So Caesar shall not find them.

CAIUS LUCIUS: Let proof speak.

CLOTEN: His majesty bids you welcome. Make
pastime with us a day or two, or longer: if
you seek us afterwards in other terms, you
shall find us in our salt-water girdle: if you
beat us out of it, it is yours; if you fall in
the adventure, our crows shall fare the better
for you; and there's an end.

CAIUS LUCIUS: So, sir.

CYMBELINE: I know your master's pleasure and he mine:
All the remain is 'Welcome!'

Exeunt

SCENE II. Another room in the palace.

Enter PISANIO, with a letter

PISANIO: How? of adultery? Wherefore write you not
What monster's her accuser? Leonatus,
O master! what a strange infection
Is fall'n into thy ear! What false Italian,
As poisonous-tongued as handed, hath prevail'd
On thy too ready hearing? Disloyal! No:
She's punish'd for her truth, and undergoes,
More goddess-like than wife-like, such assaults
As would take in some virtue. O my master!
Thy mind to her is now as low as were
Thy fortunes. How! that I should murder her?
Upon the love and truth and vows which I
Have made to thy command? I, her? her blood?
If it be so to do good service, never
Let me be counted serviceable. How look I,
That I should seem to lack humanity
so much as this fact comes to?

Reading

'Do't: the letter
that I have sent her, by her own command
Shall give thee opportunity.' O damn'd paper!
Black as the ink that's on thee! Senseless bauble,
Art thou a feodary for this act, and look'st
So virgin-like without? Lo, here she comes.

I am ignorant in what I am commanded.

Enter IMOGEN

IMOGEN: How now, PISANIO!

PISANIO: Madam, here is a letter from my lord.

IMOGEN: Who? thy lord? that is my lord, Leonatus!
O, learn'd indeed were that astronomer
That knew the stars as I his characters;
He'ld lay the future open. You good gods,
Let what is here contain'd relish of love,
Of my lord's health, of his content, yet not
That we two are asunder; let that grieve him:
Some griefs are med'cinable; that is one of them,
For it doth physic love: of his content,
All but in that! Good wax, thy leave. Blest be
You bees that make these locks of counsel! Lovers
And men in dangerous bonds pray not alike:
Though forfeiters you cast in prison, yet
You clasp young Cupid's tables. Good news, gods!

Reads

'Justice, and your father's wrath, should he take me
in his dominion, could not be so cruel to me, as
you, O the dearest of creatures, would even renew me
with your eyes. Take notice that I am in Cambria,
at Milford-Haven: what your own love will out of

this advise you, follow. So he wishes you all
happiness, that remains loyal to his vow, and your,
increasing in love, LEONATUS POSTHUMUS.'
O, for a horse with wings! Hear'st thou, PISANIO?
He is at Milford-Haven: read, and tell me
How far 'tis thither. If one of mean affairs
May plod it in a week, why may not I
Glide thither in a day? Then, true PISANIO,--
Who long'st, like me, to see thy lord; who long'st,--
let me bate,-but not like me--yet long'st,
But in a fainter kind:--O, not like me;
For mine's beyond beyond--say, and speak thick;
Love's counsellor should fill the bores of hearing,
To the smothering of the sense--how far it is
To this same blessed Milford: and by the way
Tell me how Wales was made so happy as
To inherit such a haven: but first of all,
How we may steal from hence, and for the gap
That we shall make in time, from our hence-going
And our return, to excuse: but first, how get hence:
Why should excuse be born or e'er begot?
We'll talk of that hereafter. Prithee, speak,
How many score of miles may we well ride
'Twixt hour and hour?

PISANIO: One score 'twixt sun and sun,
Madam, 's enough for you:

Aside

and too much too.

IMOGEN: Why, one that rode to's execution, man,
Could never go so slow: I have heard of
riding wagers, Where horses have been nimbler than the sands That run i' the clock's behalf. But this is foolery:
Go bid my woman feign a sickness; say
She'll home to her father: and provide me presently
A riding-suit, no costlier than would fit
A franklin's housewife.

PISANIO: Madam, you're best consider.

IMOGEN: I see before me, man: nor here, nor here,
Nor what ensues, but have a fog in them,
That I cannot look through. Away, I prithee;
Do as I bid thee: there's no more to say,
Accessible is none but Milford way.

Exeunt

SCENE III. Wales: a mountainous country with a cave.

Enter, from the cave, BELARIUS; GUIDERIUS, and ARVIRAGUS following

BELARIUS: A goodly day not to keep house, with such
Whose roof's as low as ours! Stoop, boys; this gate
Instructs you how to adore the heavens and bows you

To a morning's holy office: the gates of monarchs
Are arch'd so high that giants may jet through
And keep their impious turbans on, without
Good morrow to the sun. Hail, thou fair heaven!
We house i' the rock, yet use thee not so hardly
As prouder livers do.

GUIDERIUS: Hail, heaven!

ARVIRAGUS: Hail, heaven!

BELARIUS: Now for our mountain sport: up to yond hill;
Your legs are young; I'll tread these flats. Consider,
When you above perceive me like a crow,
That it is place which lessens and sets off;
And you may then revolve what tales I have told you
Of courts, of princes, of the tricks in war:
This service is not service, so being done,
But being so allow'd: to apprehend thus,
Draws us a profit from all things we see;
And often, to our comfort, shall we find
The sharded beetle in a safer hold
Than is the full-wing'd eagle. O, this life
Is nobler than attending for a cheque,
Richer than doing nothing for a bauble,
Prouder than rustling in unpaid-for silk:
Such gain the cap of him that makes 'em fine,
Yet keeps his book uncross'd: no life to ours.

GUIDERIUS: Out of your proof you speak: we, poor unfledged, Have never wing'd from view o' the nest, nor know not What air's from home. Haply this life is best,
If quiet life be best; sweeter to you
That have a sharper known; well corresponding
With your stiff age: but unto us it is
A cell of ignorance; travelling a-bed;
A prison for a debtor, that not dares
To stride a limit.

ARVIRAGUS: What should we speak of
When we are old as you? when we shall hear
The rain and wind beat dark December, how,
In this our pinching cave, shall we discourse
The freezing hours away? We have seen nothing;
We are beastly, subtle as the fox for prey,
Like warlike as the wolf for what we eat;
Our valour is to chase what flies; our cage
We make a quire, as doth the prison'd bird,
And sing our bondage freely.

BELARIUS: How you speak!
Did you but know the city's usuries
And felt them knowingly; the art o' the court
As hard to leave as keep; whose top to climb
Is certain falling, or so slippery that
The fear's as bad as falling; the toil o' the war,
A pain that only seems to seek out danger
I' the name of fame and honour; which dies i'
the search, And hath as oft a slanderous epitaph

As record of fair act; nay, many times,
Doth ill deserve by doing well; what's worse,
Must court'sy at the censure:--O boys, this story
The world may read in me: my body's mark'd
With Roman swords, and my report was once
First with the best of note: Cymbeline loved me,
And when a soldier was the theme, my name
Was not far off: then was I as a tree
Whose boughs did bend with fruit: but in one night,
A storm or robbery, call it what you will,
Shook down my mellow hangings, nay, my leaves,
And left me bare to weather.

GUIDERIUS: Uncertain favour!

BELARIUS: My fault being nothing--as I have told you oft--
But that two villains, whose false oaths prevail'd
Before my perfect honour, swore to Cymbeline
I was confederate with the Romans: so
Follow'd my banishment, and this twenty years
This rock and these demesnes have been my world;
Where I have lived at honest freedom, paid
More pious debts to heaven than in all
The fore-end of my time. But up to the mountains!
This is not hunters' language: he that strikes
The venison first shall be the lord o' the feast;
To him the other two shall minister;
And we will fear no poison, which attends
In place of greater state. I'll meet you in the valleys.

Exeunt GUIDERIUS and ARVIRAGUS

How hard it is to hide the sparks of nature!
These boys know little they are sons to the king;
Nor Cymbeline dreams that they are alive.
They think they are mine; and though train'd
up thus meanly I' the cave wherein they bow, their thoughts do
hit The roofs of palaces, and nature prompts them
In simple and low things to prince it much
Beyond the trick of others. This Polydore,
The heir of Cymbeline and Britain, who
The king his father call'd Guiderius,--Jove!
When on my three-foot stool I sit and tell
The warlike feats I have done, his spirits fly out
Into my story: say 'Thus, mine enemy fell,
And thus I set my foot on 's neck;' even then
The princely blood flows in his cheek, he sweats,
Strains his young nerves and puts himself in posture
That acts my words. The younger brother, Cadwal,
Once Arviragus, in as like a figure,
Strikes life into my speech and shows much more
His own conceiving.--Hark, the game is roused!
O Cymbeline! heaven and my conscience knows
Thou didst unjustly banish me: whereon,
At three and two years old, I stole these babes;
Thinking to bar thee of succession, as
Thou reft'st me of my lands. Euriphile,
Thou wast their nurse; they took thee for
their mother, And every day do honour to her grave:
Myself, Belarius, that am Morgan call'd,

They take for natural father. The game is up.

Exit

SCENE IV. Country near Milford-Haven.

Enter PISANIO and IMOGEN

IMOGEN: Thou told'st me, when we came from horse, the place Was near at hand: ne'er long'd my mother so
To see me first, as I have now. PISANIO! man!
Where is Posthumus? What is in thy mind,
That makes thee stare thus? Wherefore breaks that sigh
From the inward of thee? One, but painted thus,
Would be interpreted a thing perplex'd
Beyond self-explication: put thyself
Into a havior of less fear, ere wildness
Vanquish my staider senses. What's the matter?
Why tender'st thou that paper to me, with
A look untender? If't be summer news,
Smile to't before; if winterly, thou need'st
But keep that countenance still. My husband's hand!
That drug-damn'd Italy hath out-craftied him,
And he's at some hard point. Speak, man: thy tongue
May take off some extremity, which to read
Would be even mortal to me.

PISANIO: Please you, read; And you shall find me, wretched man, a thing The most disdain'd of fortune.

IMOGEN: *[Reads]* 'Thy mistress, PISANIO, hath played the strumpet in my bed; the testimonies whereof lie bleeding in me. I speak not out of weak surmises, but from proof as strong as my grief and as certain as I expect my revenge. That part thou, PISANIO, must act for me, if thy faith be not tainted with the breach of hers. Let thine own hands take away her life: I shall give thee opportunity at Milford-Haven. She hath my letter for the purpose where, if thou fear to strike and to make me certain it is done, thou art the pandar to her dishonour and equally to me disloyal.'

PISANIO: What shall I need to draw my sword? the paper
Hath cut her throat already. No, 'tis slander,
Whose edge is sharper than the sword, whose tongue
Outvenoms all the worms of Nile, whose breath
Rides on the posting winds and doth belie
All corners of the world: kings, queens and states,
Maids, matrons, nay, the secrets of the grave
This viperous slander enters. What cheer, madam?

IMOGEN: False to his bed! What is it to be false?
To lie in watch there and to think on him?
To weep 'twixt clock and clock? if sleep
charge nature, To break it with a fearful dream of him
And cry myself awake? that's false to's bed, is it?

PISANIO: Alas, good lady!

IMOGEN: I false! Thy conscience witness: Iachimo,
Thou didst accuse him of incontinency;
Thou then look'dst like a villain; now methinks
Thy favour's good enough. Some jay of Italy
Whose mother was her painting, hath betray'd him:
Poor I am stale, a garment out of fashion;
And, for I am richer than to hang by the walls,
I must be ripp'd:--to pieces with me!--O,
Men's vows are women's traitors! All good seeming,
By thy revolt, O husband, shall be thought
Put on for villany; not born where't grows,
But worn a bait for ladies.

PISANIO: Good madam, hear me.

IMOGEN: True honest men being heard, like false Aeneas,
Were in his time thought false, and Sinon's weeping
Did scandal many a holy tear, took pity
From most true wretchedness: so thou, Posthumus,
Wilt lay the leaven on all proper men;
Goodly and gallant shall be false and perjured
From thy great fall. Come, fellow, be thou honest:
Do thou thy master's bidding: when thou see'st him,
A little witness my obedience: look!
I draw the sword myself: take it, and hit
The innocent mansion of my love, my heart;
Fear not; 'tis empty of all things but grief;
Thy master is not there, who was indeed
The riches of it: do his bidding; strike

Thou mayst be valiant in a better cause;
But now thou seem'st a coward.

PISANIO: Hence, vile instrument!
Thou shalt not damn my hand.

IMOGEN: Why, I must die; And if I do not by thy hand, thou art
No servant of thy master's. Against self-slaughter
There is a prohibition so divine
That cravens my weak hand. Come, here's my heart.
Something's afore't. Soft, soft! we'll no defence;
Obedient as the scabbard. What is here?
The scriptures of the loyal Leonatus,
All turn'd to heresy? Away, away,
Corrupters of my faith! you shall no more
Be stomachers to my heart. Thus may poor fools
Believe false teachers: though those that
are betray'd Do feel the treason sharply, yet the traitor
Stands in worse case of woe.
And thou, Posthumus, thou that didst set up
My disobedience 'gainst the king my father
And make me put into contempt the suits
Of princely fellows, shalt hereafter find
It is no act of common passage, but
A strain of rareness: and I grieve myself
To think, when thou shalt be disedged by her
That now thou tirest on, how thy memory
Will then be pang'd by me. Prithee, dispatch:
The lamb entreats the butcher: where's thy knife?
Thou art too slow to do thy master's bidding,

When I desire it too.

PISANIO: O gracious lady, Since I received command to do this business I have not slept one wink.

IMOGEN: Do't, and to bed then.

PISANIO: I'll wake mine eye-balls blind first.

IMOGEN: Wherefore then Didst undertake it? Why hast thou abused So many miles with a pretence? this place?
Mine action and thine own? our horses' labour?
The time inviting thee? the perturb'd court,
For my being absent? whereunto I never
Purpose return. Why hast thou gone so far,
To be unbent when thou hast ta'en thy stand,
The elected deer before thee?

PISANIO: But to win time
To lose so bad employment; in the which
I have consider'd of a course. Good lady,
Hear me with patience.

IMOGEN: Talk thy tongue weary; speak
I have heard I am a strumpet; and mine ear
Therein false struck, can take no greater wound,
Nor tent to bottom that. But speak.

PISANIO: Then, madam,
I thought you would not back again.

IMOGEN: Most like;
Bringing me here to kill me.

PISANIO: Not so, neither:
But if I were as wise as honest, then
My purpose would prove well. It cannot be
But that my master is abused:
Some villain, ay, and singular in his art.
Hath done you both this cursed injury.

IMOGEN: Some Roman courtezan.

PISANIO: No, on my life.
I'll give but notice you are dead and send him
Some bloody sign of it; for 'tis commanded
I should do so: you shall be miss'd at court,
And that will well confirm it.

IMOGEN: Why good fellow,
What shall I do the where? where bide? how live?
Or in my life what comfort, when I am
Dead to my husband?

PISANIO: If you'll back to the court--

IMOGEN: No court, no father; nor no more ado
With that harsh, noble, simple nothing,
That Cloten, whose love-suit hath been to me
As fearful as a siege.

PISANIO: If not at court, Then not in Britain must you bide.

IMOGEN: Where then
Hath Britain all the sun that shines? Day, night,
Are they not but in Britain? I' the world's volume
Our Britain seems as of it, but not in 't;
In a great pool a swan's nest: prithee, think
There's livers out of Britain.

PISANIO: I am most glad
You think of other place. The ambassador,
Lucius the Roman, comes to Milford-Haven
To-morrow: now, if you could wear a mind
Dark as your fortune is, and but disguise
That which, to appear itself, must not yet be
But by self-danger, you should tread a course
Pretty and full of view; yea, haply, near
The residence of Posthumus; so nigh at least
That though his actions were not visible, yet
Report should render him hourly to your ear
As truly as he moves.

IMOGEN: O, for such means!
Though peril to my modesty, not death on't,
I would adventure.

PISANIO: Well, then, here's the point:
You must forget to be a woman; change
Command into obedience: fear and niceness--

The handmaids of all women, or, more truly,
Woman its pretty self--into a waggish courage:
Ready in gibes, quick-answer'd, saucy and
As quarrelous as the weasel; nay, you must
Forget that rarest treasure of your cheek,
Exposing it--but, O, the harder heart!
Alack, no remedy!--to the greedy touch
Of common-kissing Titan, and forget
Your laboursome and dainty trims, wherein
You made great Juno angry.

IMOGEN: Nay, be brief I see into thy end, and am almost
A man already.

PISANIO: First, make yourself but like one.
Fore-thinking this, I have already fit--
'Tis in my cloak-bag--doublet, hat, hose, all
That answer to them: would you in their serving,
And with what imitation you can borrow
From youth of such a season, 'fore noble Lucius
Present yourself, desire his service, tell him
wherein you're happy,--which you'll make him know,
If that his head have ear in music,--doubtless
With joy he will embrace you, for he's honourable
And doubling that, most holy. Your means abroad,
You have me, rich; and I will never fail
Beginning nor supplyment.

IMOGEN: Thou art all the comfort
The gods will diet me with. Prithee, away:

There's more to be consider'd; but we'll even
All that good time will give us: this attempt
I am soldier to, and will abide it with
A prince's courage. Away, I prithee.

PISANIO: Well, madam, we must take a short farewell,
Lest, being miss'd, I be suspected of
Your carriage from the court. My noble mistress,
Here is a box; I had it from the queen:
What's in't is precious; if you are sick at sea,
Or stomach-qualm'd at land, a dram of this
Will drive away distemper. To some shade,
And fit you to your manhood. May the gods
Direct you to the best!

IMOGEN: Amen: I thank thee.

Exeunt, severally

SCENE V. A room in Cymbeline's palace.

Enter CYMBELINE, QUEEN, CLOTEN, LUCIUS, Lords, and Attendants

CYMBELINE: Thus far; and so farewell.

CAIUS LUCIUS: Thanks, royal sir.
My emperor hath wrote, I must from hence;
And am right sorry that I must report ye

My master's enemy.

CYMBELINE: Our subjects, sir,
Will not endure his yoke; and for ourself
To show less sovereignty than they, must needs
Appear unkinglike.

CAIUS LUCIUS: So, sir: I desire of you
A conduct over-land to Milford-Haven.
Madam, all joy befal your grace!

QUEEN: And you!

CYMBELINE: My lords, you are appointed for that office;
The due of honour in no point omit.
So farewell, noble Lucius.

CAIUS LUCIUS: Your hand, my lord.

CLOTEN: Receive it friendly; but from this time forth
I wear it as your enemy.

CAIUS LUCIUS: Sir, the event
Is yet to name the winner: fare you well.

CYMBELINE: Leave not the worthy Lucius, good my lords,
Till he have cross'd the Severn. Happiness!

Exeunt LUCIUS and Lords

QUEEN: He goes hence frowning: but it honours us
That we have given him cause.

CLOTEN: 'Tis all the better;
Your valiant Britons have their wishes in it.

CYMBELINE: Lucius hath wrote already to the emperor
How it goes here. It fits us therefore ripely
Our chariots and our horsemen be in readiness:
The powers that he already hath in Gallia
Will soon be drawn to head, from whence he moves
His war for Britain.

QUEEN: 'Tis not sleepy business;
But must be look'd to speedily and strongly.

CYMBELINE: Our expectation that it would be thus
Hath made us forward. But, my gentle queen,
Where is our daughter? She hath not appear'd
Before the Roman, nor to us hath tender'd
The duty of the day: she looks us like
A thing more made of malice than of duty:
We have noted it. Call her before us; for
We have been too slight in sufferance.

Exit an Attendant

QUEEN: Royal sir, Since the exile of Posthumus, most retired
Hath her life been; the cure whereof, my lord,
'Tis time must do. Beseech your majesty,

Forbear sharp speeches to her: she's a lady
So tender of rebukes that words are strokes
And strokes death to her.

Re-enter Attendant

CYMBELINE: Where is she, sir? How
Can her contempt be answer'd?

Attendant: Please you, sir,
Her chambers are all lock'd; and there's no answer
That will be given to the loudest noise we make.

QUEEN: My lord, when last I went to visit her,
She pray'd me to excuse her keeping close,
Whereto constrain'd by her infirmity,
She should that duty leave unpaid to you,
Which daily she was bound to proffer: this
She wish'd me to make known; but our great court
Made me to blame in memory.

CYMBELINE: Her doors lock'd? Not seen of late? Grant, heavens, that which I fear Prove false!

Exit

QUEEN: Son, I say, follow the king.

CLOTEN: That man of hers, PISANIO, her old servant, have not seen these two days.

QUEEN: Go, look after.

Exit CLOTEN

PISANIO, thou that stand'st so for Posthumus!
He hath a drug of mine; I pray his absence
Proceed by swallowing that, for he believes
It is a thing most precious. But for her,
Where is she gone? Haply, despair hath seized her,
Or, wing'd with fervor of her love, she's flown
To her desired Posthumus: gone she is
To death or to dishonour; and my end
Can make good use of either: she being down,
I have the placing of the British crown.

Re-enter CLOTEN

How now, my son!

CLOTEN: 'Tis certain she is fled.
Go in and cheer the king: he rages; none
Dare come about him.

QUEEN: *[Aside]* All the better: may
This night forestall him of the coming day!

Exit

CLOTEN: I love and hate her: for she's fair and royal,

And that she hath all courtly parts more exquisite
Than lady, ladies, woman; from every one
The best she hath, and she, of all compounded,
Outsells them all; I love her therefore: but
Disdaining me and throwing favours on
The low Posthumus slanders so her judgment
That what's else rare is choked; and in that point
I will conclude to hate her, nay, indeed,
To be revenged upon her. For when fools Shall—

Enter PISANIO

Who is here? What, are you packing, sirrah?
Come hither: ah, you precious pander! Villain,
Where is thy lady? In a word; or else
Thou art straightway with the fiends.

PISANIO: O, good my lord!

CLOTEN: Where is thy lady? Or, by Jupiter,--
I will not ask again. Close villain,
I'll have this secret from thy heart, or rip
Thy heart to find it. Is she with Posthumus?
From whose so many weights of baseness cannot
A dram of worth be drawn.

PISANIO: Alas, my lord,
How can she be with him? When was she missed?
He is in Rome.

CLOTEN: Where is she, sir? Come nearer;
No further halting: satisfy me home
What is become of her.

PISANIO: O, my all-worthy lord!

CLOTEN: All-worthy villain!
Discover where thy mistress is at once,
At the next word: no more of 'worthy lord!'
Speak, or thy silence on the instant is
Thy condemnation and thy death.

PISANIO: Then, sir, This paper is the history of my knowledge
Touching her flight.

Presenting a letter

CLOTEN: Let's see't. I will pursue her
Even to Augustus' throne.

PISANIO: *[Aside]* Or this, or perish.
She's far enough; and what he learns by this
May prove his travel, not her danger.

CLOTEN: Hum!

PISANIO: *[Aside]* I'll write to my lord she's dead. O Imogen,
Safe mayst thou wander, safe return again!

CLOTEN: Sirrah, is this letter true?

PISANIO: Sir, as I think.

CLOTEN: It is Posthumus' hand; I know't. Sirrah, if thou wouldst not be a villain, but do me true service, undergo those employments wherein I should have cause to use thee with a serious industry, that is, what villany soe'er I bid thee do, to perform it directly and truly, I would think thee an honest man: thou shouldst neither want my means for thy relief nor my voice for thy preferment.

PISANIO: Well, my good lord.

CLOTEN: Wilt thou serve me? for since patiently and constantly thou hast stuck to the bare fortune of that beggar Posthumus, thou canst not, in the course of gratitude, but be a diligent follower of mine: wilt thou serve me?

PISANIO: Sir, I will.

CLOTEN: Give me thy hand; here's my purse. Hast any of thy late master's garments in thy possession?

PISANIO: I have, my lord, at my lodging, the same suit he wore when he took leave of my lady and mistress.

CLOTEN: The first service thou dost me, fetch that suit hither: let it be thy lint service; go.

PISANIO: I shall, my lord.

Exit

CLOTEN: Meet thee at Milford-Haven!--I forgot to ask him one thing; I'll remember't anon:--even there, thou villain Posthumus, will I kill thee. I would these garments were come. She said upon a time--the bitterness of it I now belch from my heart--that she held the very garment of Posthumus in more respect than my noble and natural person together with the adornment of my qualities. With that suit upon my back, will I ravish her: first kill him, and in her eyes; there shall she see my valour, which will then be a torment to her contempt. He on the ground, my speech of insultment ended on his dead body, and when my lust hath dined,--which, as I say, to vex her I will execute in the clothes that she so praised,--to the court I'll knock her back, foot her home again. She hath despised me rejoicingly, and I'll be merry in my revenge.

Re-enter PISANIO, with the clothes

Be those the garments?

PISANIO: Ay, my noble lord.

CLOTEN: How long is't since she went to Milford-Haven?

PISANIO: She can scarce be there yet.

CLOTEN: Bring this apparel to my chamber; that is the second thing that I have commanded thee: the third is, that thou wilt be a voluntary mute to my design. Be but duteous, and true preferment shall tender itself to thee. My revenge is now at Milford: would I had wings to follow it! Come, and be true.

Exit

PISANIO: Thou bid'st me to my loss: for true to thee
Were to prove false, which I will never be,
To him that is most true. To Milford go,
And find not her whom thou pursuest. Flow, flow,
You heavenly blessings, on her! This fool's speed
Be cross'd with slowness; labour be his meed!

Exit

SCENE VI. Wales. Before the cave of Belarius.

Enter IMOGEN, in boy's clothes

IMOGEN: I see a man's life is a tedious one:
I have tired myself, and for two nights together
Have made the ground my bed. I should be sick,
But that my resolution helps me. Milford,

When from the mountain-top PISANIO show'd thee,
Thou wast within a ken: O Jove! I think
Foundations fly the wretched; such, I mean,
Where they should be relieved. Two beggars told me
I could not miss my way: will poor folks lie,
That have afflictions on them, knowing 'tis
A punishment or trial? Yes; no wonder,
When rich ones scarce tell true. To lapse in fulness
Is sorer than to lie for need, and falsehood
Is worse in kings than beggars. My dear lord!
Thou art one o' the false ones. Now I think on thee,
My hunger's gone; but even before, I was
At point to sink for food. But what is this?
Here is a path to't: 'tis some savage hold:
I were best not to call; I dare not call:
yet famine, Ere clean it o'erthrow nature, makes it valiant,
Plenty and peace breeds cowards: hardness ever
Of hardiness is mother. Ho! who's here?
If any thing that's civil, speak; if savage,
Take or lend. Ho! No answer? Then I'll enter.
Best draw my sword: and if mine enemy
But fear the sword like me, he'll scarcely look on't.
Such a foe, good heavens!

Exit, to the cave

Enter BELARIUS, GUIDERIUS, and ARVIRAGUS

BELARIUS: You, Polydote, have proved best woodman and
Are master of the feast: Cadwal and I

Will play the cook and servant; 'tis our match:
The sweat of industry would dry and die,
But for the end it works to. Come; our stomachs
Will make what's homely savoury: weariness
Can snore upon the flint, when resty sloth
Finds the down pillow hard. Now peace be here,
Poor house, that keep'st thyself!

GUIDERIUS: I am thoroughly weary.

ARVIRAGUS: I am weak with toil, yet strong in appetite.

GUIDERIUS: There is cold meat i' the cave; we'll browse on that, Whilst what we have kill'd be cook'd.

BELARIUS: *[Looking into the cave]*
Stay; come not in. But that it eats our victuals, I should think
Here were a fairy.

GUIDERIUS: What's the matter, sir?

BELARIUS: By Jupiter, an angel! or, if not,
An earthly paragon! Behold divineness
No elder than a boy!

Re-enter IMOGEN

IMOGEN: Good masters, harm me not:
Before I enter'd here, I call'd; and thought
To have begg'd or bought what I have took:

good troth, I have stol'n nought, nor would not, though I had found Gold strew'd i' the floor. Here's money for my meat:
I would have left it on the board so soon
As I had made my meal, and parted
With prayers for the provider.

GUIDERIUS: Money, youth?

ARVIRAGUS: All gold and silver rather turn to dirt!
As 'tis no better reckon'd, but of those
Who worship dirty gods.

IMOGEN: I see you're angry:
Know, if you kill me for my fault, I should
Have died had I not made it.

BELARIUS: Whither bound?

IMOGEN: To Milford-Haven.

BELARIUS: What's your name?

IMOGEN: Fidele, sir. I have a kinsman who
Is bound for Italy; he embark'd at Milford;
To whom being going, almost spent with hunger,
I am fall'n in this offence.

BELARIUS: Prithee, fair youth,
Think us no churls, nor measure our good minds
By this rude place we live in. Well encounter'd!

'Tis almost night: you shall have better cheer
Ere you depart: and thanks to stay and eat it.
Boys, bid him welcome.

GUIDERIUS: Were you a woman, youth,
I should woo hard but be your groom. In honesty,
I bid for you as I'd buy.

ARVIRAGUS: I'll make't my comfort
He is a man; I'll love him as my brother:
And such a welcome as I'd give to him
After long absence, such is yours: most welcome!
Be sprightly, for you fall 'mongst friends.

IMOGEN: 'Mongst friends, If brothers.

Aside

Would it had been so, that they
Had been my father's sons! then had my prize
Been less, and so more equal ballasting
To thee, Posthumus.

BELARIUS: He wrings at some distress.

GUIDERIUS: Would I could free't!

ARVIRAGUS: Or I, whate'er it be,
What pain it cost, what danger. God's!

BELARIUS: Hark, boys.

Whispering

IMOGEN: Great men,
That had a court no bigger than this cave,
That did attend themselves and had the virtue
Which their own conscience seal'd them--laying by
That nothing-gift of differing multitudes--
Could not out-peer these twain. Pardon me, gods!
I'd change my sex to be companion with them,
Since Leonatus's false.

BELARIUS: It shall be so.
Boys, we'll go dress our hunt. Fair youth, come in:
Discourse is heavy, fasting; when we have supp'd,
We'll mannerly demand thee of thy story,
So far as thou wilt speak it.

GUIDERIUS: Pray, draw near.

ARVIRAGUS: The night to the owl and morn to the lark less welcome.

IMOGEN: Thanks, sir.

ARVIRAGUS: I pray, draw near.

Exeunt

SCENE VII. Rome. A public place.

Enter two Senators and Tribunes

First Senator: This is the tenor of the emperor's writ:
That since the common men are now in action
'Gainst the Pannonians and Dalmatians,
And that the legions now in Gallia are
Full weak to undertake our wars against
The fall'n-off Britons, that we do incite
The gentry to this business. He creates
Lucius preconsul: and to you the tribunes,
For this immediate levy, he commends
His absolute commission. Long live Caesar!

First Tribune: Is Lucius general of the forces?

Second Senator: Ay.

First Tribune: Remaining now in Gallia?

First Senator: With those legions
Which I have spoke of, whereunto your levy
Must be supplyant: the words of your commission
Will tie you to the numbers and the time
Of their dispatch.

First Tribune: We will discharge our duty.

Exeunt

ACT IV. SCENE I. Wales: near the cave of Belarius.

Enter CLOTEN

CLOTEN: I am near to the place where they should meet, if

PISANIO: have mapped it truly. How fit his garments serve me! Why should his mistress, who was made by him that made the tailor, not be fit too? the rather--saving reverence of the word--for 'tis said a woman's fitness comes by fits. Therein I must play the workman. I dare speak it to myself--for it is not vain-glory for a man and his glass to confer in his own chamber--I mean, the lines of my body are as well drawn as his; no less young, more strong, not beneath him in fortunes, beyond him in the advantage of the time, above him in birth, alike conversant in general services, and more remarkable in single oppositions: yet this imperceiverant thing loves him in my despite. What mortality is! Posthumus, thy head, which now is growing upon thy shoulders, shall within this hour be off; thy mistress enforced; thy garments cut to pieces before thy face: and all this done, spurn her home to her father; who may haply be a little angry for my so rough usage; but my mother, having power of his testiness, shall turn all into my commendations. My horse is tied up safe: out, sword, and to a sore purpose! Fortune, put them into my hand! This is the very description of their meeting-place; and the fellow dares not deceive me.

Exit

SCENE II. Before the cave of Belarius.

Enter, from the cave, BELARIUS, GUIDERIUS, ARVIRAGUS, and IMOGEN

BELARIUS: *[To IMOGEN]* You are not well: remain here in the cave; We'll come to you after hunting.

ARVIRAGUS: *[To IMOGEN]* Brother, stay here
Are we not brothers?

IMOGEN: So man and man should be;
But clay and clay differs in dignity,
Whose dust is both alike. I am very sick.

GUIDERIUS: Go you to hunting; I'll abide with him.

IMOGEN: So sick I am not, yet I am not well;
But not so citizen a wanton as To seem to die ere sick:
so please you, leave me; Stick to your journal course:
the breach of custom Is breach of all.
I am ill, but your being by me

Cannot amend me; society is no comfort
To one not sociable: I am not very sick,
Since I can reason of it. Pray you, trust me here:
I'll rob none but myself; and let me die,
Stealing so poorly.

GUIDERIUS: I love thee; I have spoke it
How much the quantity, the weight as much,
As I do love my father.

BELARIUS: What! how! how!

ARVIRAGUS: If it be sin to say so, I yoke me
In my good brother's fault: I know not why
I love this youth; and I have heard you say,
Love's reason's without reason: the bier at door,
And a demand who is't shall die, I'd say
'My father, not this youth.'

BELARIUS: *[Aside]* O noble strain!
O worthiness of nature! breed of greatness!
Cowards father cowards and base things sire base:
Nature hath meal and bran, contempt and grace.
I'm not their father; yet who this should be,
Doth miracle itself, loved before me.
'Tis the ninth hour o' the morn.

ARVIRAGUS: Brother, farewell.

IMOGEN: I wish ye sport.

ARVIRAGUS: You health. So please you, sir.

IMOGEN: *[Aside]* These are kind creatures. Gods, what lies
I have heard! Our courtiers say all's savage but at court:
Experience, O, thou disprovest report!
The imperious seas breed monsters, for the dish
Poor tributary rivers as sweet fish.
I am sick still; heart-sick.PISANIO, I'll now taste of thy drug.

Swallows some

GUIDERIUS: I could not stir him:
He said he was gentle, but unfortunate;
Dishonestly afflicted, but yet honest.

ARVIRAGUS: Thus did he answer me: yet said, hereafter
I might know more.

BELARIUS: To the field, to the field!
We'll leave you for this time: go in and rest.

ARVIRAGUS: We'll not be long away.

BELARIUS: Pray, be not sick,
For you must be our housewife.

IMOGEN: Well or ill,
I am bound to you.

BELARIUS: And shalt be ever.

Exit IMOGEN, to the cave

This youth, how'er distress'd, appears he hath had
Good ancestors.

ARVIRAGUS: How angel-like he sings!

GUIDERIUS: But his neat cookery! he cut our roots
In characters, And sauced our broths, as Juno had been sick
And he her dieter.

ARVIRAGUS: Nobly he yokes
A smiling with a sigh, as if the sigh
Was that it was, for not being such a smile;
The smile mocking the sigh, that it would fly
From so divine a temple, to commix
With winds that sailors rail at.

GUIDERIUS: I do note That grief and patience, rooted in him both, Mingle their spurs together.

ARVIRAGUS: Grow, patience!
And let the stinking elder, grief, untwine
His perishing root with the increasing vine!

BELARIUS: It is great morning. Come, away!--
Who's there?

Enter CLOTEN

CLOTEN: I cannot find those runagates; that villain
Hath mock'd me. I am faint.

BELARIUS: 'Those runagates!'
Means he not us? I partly know him: 'tis
Cloten, the son o' the queen. I fear some ambush.
I saw him not these many years, and yet
I know 'tis he. We are held as outlaws: hence!

GUIDERIUS: He is but one: you and my brother search
What companies are near: pray you, away;
Let me alone with him.

Exeunt BELARIUS and ARVIRAGUS

CLOTEN: Soft! What are you
That fly me thus? some villain mountaineers?
I have heard of such. What slave art thou?

GUIDERIUS: A thing
More slavish did I ne'er than answering
A slave without a knock.

CLOTEN: Thou art a robber,
A law-breaker, a villain: yield thee, thief.

GUIDERIUS: To who? to thee? What art thou? Have not I
An arm as big as thine? a heart as big?

Thy words, I grant, are bigger, for I wear not
My dagger in my mouth. Say what thou art,
Why I should yield to thee?

CLOTEN: Thou villain base,
Know'st me not by my clothes?

GUIDERIUS: No, nor thy tailor, rascal,
Who is thy grandfather: he made those clothes,
Which, as it seems, make thee.

CLOTEN: Thou precious varlet,
My tailor made them not.

GUIDERIUS: Hence, then, and thank
The man that gave them thee. Thou art some fool;
I am loath to beat thee.

CLOTEN: Thou injurious thief,
Hear but my name, and tremble.

GUIDERIUS: What's thy name?

CLOTEN: Cloten, thou villain.

GUIDERIUS: Cloten, thou double villain, be thy name,
I cannot tremble at it: were it Toad, or
Adder, Spider, 'Twould move me sooner.

CLOTEN: To thy further fear,

Nay, to thy mere confusion, thou shalt know
I am son to the queen.

GUIDERIUS: I am sorry for 't; not seeming
So worthy as thy birth.

CLOTEN: Art not afeard?

GUIDERIUS: Those that I reverence those I fear, the wise:
At fools I laugh, not fear them.

CLOTEN: Die the death: When I have slain thee with my
proper hand, I'll follow those that even now fled hence,
And on the gates of Lud's-town set your heads:
Yield, rustic mountaineer.

Exeunt, fighting

Re-enter BELARIUS and ARVIRAGUS

BELARIUS: No companies abroad?

ARVIRAGUS: None in the world: you did mistake him, sure.

BELARIUS: I cannot tell: long is it since I saw him,
But time hath nothing blurr'd those lines of favour
Which then he wore; the snatches in his voice,
And burst of speaking, were as his: I am absolute
'Twas very Cloten.

ARVIRAGUS: In this place we left them:
I wish my brother make good time with him,
You say he is so fell.

BELARIUS: Being scarce made up,
I mean, to man, he had not apprehension
Of roaring terrors; for the effect of judgment
Is oft the cause of fear. But, see, thy brother.

Re-enter GUIDERIUS, with CLOTEN'S head

GUIDERIUS: This Cloten was a fool, an empty purse;
There was no money in't: not Hercules
Could have knock'd out his brains, for he had none:
Yet I not doing this, the fool had borne
My head as I do his.

BELARIUS: What hast thou done?

GUIDERIUS: I am perfect what: cut off one Cloten's head,
Son to the queen, after his own report;
Who call'd me traitor, mountaineer, and swore
With his own single hand he'ld take us in
Displace our heads where--thank the gods!--they grow,
And set them on Lud's-town.

BELARIUS: We are all undone.

GUIDERIUS: Why, worthy father, what have we to lose,
But that he swore to take, our lives? The law

Protects not us: then why should we be tender
To let an arrogant piece of flesh threat us,
Play judge and executioner all himself,
For we do fear the law? What company
Discover you abroad?

BELARIUS: No single soul
Can we set eye on; but in all safe reason
He must have some attendants. Though his humour
Was nothing but mutation, ay, and that
From one bad thing to worse; not frenzy, not
Absolute madness could so far have raved
To bring him here alone; although perhaps
It may be heard at court that such as we
Cave here, hunt here, are outlaws, and in time
May make some stronger head; the which he hearing--
As it is like him--might break out, and swear
He'ld fetch us in; yet is't not probable
To come alone, either he so undertaking,
Or they so suffering: then on good ground we fear,
If we do fear this body hath a tail
More perilous than the head.

ARVIRAGUS: Let ordinance
Come as the gods foresay it: howsoe'er,
My brother hath done well.

BELARIUS: I had no mind
To hunt this day: the boy Fidele's sickness
Did make my way long forth.

GUIDERIUS: With his own sword,
Which he did wave against my throat, I have ta'en
His head from him: I'll throw't into the creek
Behind our rock; and let it to the sea,
And tell the fishes he's the queen's son, Cloten:
That's all I reck.

Exit

BELARIUS: I fear 'twill be revenged:
Would, Polydote, thou hadst not done't! though valour
Becomes thee well enough.

ARVIRAGUS: Would I had done't
So the revenge alone pursued me! Polydore,
I love thee brotherly, but envy much
Thou hast robb'd me of this deed: I would revenges,
That possible strength might meet, would seek us through
And put us to our answer.

BELARIUS: Well, 'tis done:
We'll hunt no more to-day, nor seek for danger
Where there's no profit. I prithee, to our rock;
You and Fidele play the cooks: I'll stay
Till hasty Polydote return, and bring him
To dinner presently.

ARVIRAGUS: Poor sick Fidele!
I'll weringly to him: to gain his colour

I'ld let a parish of such Clotens' blood,
And praise myself for charity.

Exit

BELARIUS: O thou goddess,
Thou divine Nature, how thyself thou blazon'st
In these two princely boys! They are as gentle
As zephyrs blowing below the violet,
Not wagging his sweet head; and yet as rough,
Their royal blood enchafed, as the rudest wind,
That by the top doth take the mountain pine,
And make him stoop to the vale. 'Tis wonder
That an invisible instinct should frame them
To royalty unlearn'd, honour untaught,
Civility not seen from other, valour
That wildly grows in them, but yields a crop
As if it had been sow'd. Yet still it's strange
What Cloten's being here to us portends,
Or what his death will bring us.

Re-enter GUIDERIUS

GUIDERIUS: Where's my brother?
I have sent Cloten's clotpoll down the stream,
In embassy to his mother: his body's hostage
For his return.

Solemn music

BELARIUS: My ingenious instrument!
Hark, Polydore, it sounds! But what occasion
Hath Cadwal now to give it motion? Hark!

GUIDERIUS: Is he at home?

BELARIUS: He went hence even now.

GUIDERIUS: What does he mean? since death of my dear'st
mother it did not speak before. All solemn things
Should answer solemn accidents. The matter?
Triumphs for nothing and lamenting toys
Is jollity for apes and grief for boys.
Is Cadwal mad?

BELARIUS: Look, here he comes,
And brings the dire occasion in his arms
Of what we blame him for.
Re-enter ARVIRAGUS, with IMOGEN, as dead, bearing her in his arms

ARVIRAGUS: The bird is dead
That we have made so much on. I had rather
Have skipp'd from sixteen years of age to sixty,
To have turn'd my leaping-time into a crutch,
Than have seen this.

GUIDERIUS: O sweetest, fairest lily!
My brother wears thee not the one half so well
As when thou grew'st thyself.

BELARIUS: O melancholy!
Who ever yet could sound thy bottom? find
The ooze, to show what coast thy sluggish crare
Might easiliest harbour in? Thou blessed thing!
Jove knows what man thou mightst have made; but I,
Thou diedst, a most rare boy, of melancholy.
How found you him?

ARVIRAGUS: Stark, as you see:
Thus smiling, as some fly hid tickled slumber,
Not as death's dart, being laugh'd at; his
right cheek

Reposing on a cushion.

GUIDERIUS: Where?

ARVIRAGUS: O' the floor;
His arms thus leagued: I thought he slept, and put
My clouted brogues from off my feet, whose rudeness
Answer'd my steps too loud.

GUIDERIUS: Why, he but sleeps:
If he be gone, he'll make his grave a bed;
With female fairies will his tomb be haunted,
And worms will not come to thee.

ARVIRAGUS: With fairest flowers
Whilst summer lasts and I live here, Fidele,

I'll sweeten thy sad grave: thou shalt not lack
The flower that's like thy face, pale primrose, nor
The azured harebell, like thy veins, no, nor
The leaf of eglantine, whom not to slander,
Out-sweeten'd not thy breath: the ruddock would,
With charitable bill,--O bill, sore-shaming
Those rich-left heirs that let their fathers lie
Without a monument!--bring thee all this;
Yea, and furr'd moss besides, when flowers are none,
To winter-ground thy corse.

GUIDERIUS: Prithee, have done;
And do not play in wench-like words with that
Which is so serious. Let us bury him,
And not protract with admiration what
Is now due debt. To the grave!

ARVIRAGUS: Say, where shall's lay him?

GUIDERIUS: By good Euriphile, our mother.

ARVIRAGUS: Be't so:
And let us, Polydore, though now our voices
Have got the mannish crack, sing him to the ground,
As once our mother; use like note and words,
Save that Euriphile must be Fidele.

GUIDERIUS: Cadwal,
I cannot sing: I'll weep, and word it with thee;
For notes of sorrow out of tune are worse

Than priests and fanes that lie.

ARVIRAGUS: We'll speak it, then.

BELARIUS: Great griefs, I see, medicine the less; for Cloten
Is quite forgot. He was a queen's son, boys;
And though he came our enemy, remember
He was paid for that: though mean and
mighty, rotting
Together, have one dust, yet reverence,
That angel of the world, doth make distinction
Of place 'tween high and low. Our foe was princely
And though you took his life, as being our foe,
Yet bury him as a prince.

GUIDERIUS: Pray You, fetch him hither.
Thersites' body is as good as Ajax',
When neither are alive.

ARVIRAGUS: If you'll go fetch him,
We'll say our song the whilst. Brother, begin.

Exit BELARIUS

GUIDERIUS: Nay, Cadwal, we must lay his head to the east;
My father hath a reason for't.

ARVIRAGUS: 'Tis true.

GUIDERIUS: Come on then, and remove him.

ARVIRAGUS: So. Begin.

SONG

GUIDERIUS: Fear no more the heat o' the sun,
Nor the furious winter's rages;
Thou thy worldly task hast done,
Home art gone, and ta'en thy wages:
Golden lads and girls all must,
As chimney-sweepers, come to dust.

ARVIRAGUS: Fear no more the frown o' the great;
Thou art past the tyrant's stroke;
Care no more to clothe and eat;
To thee the reed is as the oak:
The sceptre, learning, physic, must
All follow this, and come to dust.

GUIDERIUS: Fear no more the lightning flash,

ARVIRAGUS: Nor the all-dreaded thunder-stone;

GUIDERIUS: Fear not slander, censure rash;

ARVIRAGUS: Thou hast finish'd joy and moan:

GUIDERIUS ARVIRAGUS: All lovers young, all lovers must
Consign to thee, and come to dust.

GUIDERIUS: No exorciser harm thee!

ARVIRAGUS: Nor no witchcraft charm thee!

GUIDERIUS: Ghost unlaid forbear thee!

ARVIRAGUS: Nothing ill come near thee!

GUIDERIUS ARVIRAGUS: Quiet consummation have;
And renowned be thy grave!

Re-enter BELARIUS, with the body of CLOTEN

GUIDERIUS: We have done our obsequies: come, lay him down.

BELARIUS: Here's a few flowers; but 'bout midnight, more:
The herbs that have on them cold dew o' the night
Are strewings fitt'st for graves. Upon their faces.
You were as flowers, now wither'd: even so
These herblets shall, which we upon you strew.
Come on, away: apart upon our knees.
The ground that gave them first has them again:
Their pleasures here are past, so is their pain.

Exeunt BELARIUS, GUIDERIUS, and ARVIRAGUS

IMOGEN: [Awaking] Yes, sir, to Milford-Haven; which is
the way?-- I thank you.--By yond bush?--Pray, how far thither?
'Ods pittikins! can it be six mile yet?--

I have gone all night. 'Faith, I'll lie down and sleep.
But, soft! no bedfellow!--O god s and goddesses!

Seeing the body of CLOTEN

These flowers are like the pleasures of the world; This bloody man, the care on't. I hope I dream; For so I thought I was a cave-keeper,
And cook to honest creatures: but 'tis not so;
'Twas but a bolt of nothing, shot at nothing,
Which the brain makes of fumes: our very eyes
Are sometimes like our judgments, blind. Good faith,
I tremble stiff with fear: but if there be
Yet left in heaven as small a drop of pity
As a wren's eye, fear'd gods, a part of it!
The dream's here still: even when I wake, it is
Without me, as within me; not imagined, felt.
A headless man! The garments of Posthumus!
I know the shape of's leg: this is his hand;
His foot Mercurial; his Martial thigh;
The brawns of Hercules: but his Jovial face
Murder in heaven?--How!--'Tis gone.
PISANIO , All curses madded Hecuba gave the Greeks,
And mine to boot, be darted on thee! Thou,
Conspired with that irregulous devil, Cloten,
Hast here cut off my lord. To write and read
Be henceforth treacherous! Damn'd PISANIO
Hath with his forged letters,--damn'd
PISANIO-- From this most bravest vessel of the world
Struck the main-top! O Posthumus! alas,

Where is thy head? where's that? Ay me!
where's that? PISANIO might have kill'd thee at the heart,
And left this head on. How should this be?
PISANIO? 'Tis he and Cloten: malice and lucre in them
Have laid this woe here. O, 'tis pregnant, pregnant!
The drug he gave me, which he said was precious
And cordial to me, have I not found it
Murderous to the senses? That confirms it home:
This is PISANIO's deed, and Cloten's: O!
Give colour to my pale cheek with thy blood,
That we the horrider may seem to those
Which chance to find us: O, my lord, my lord!

Falls on the body

Enter LUCIUS, a Captain and other Officers, and a Soothsayer

Captain: To them the legions garrison'd in Gailia,
After your will, have cross'd the sea, attending
You here at Milford-Haven with your ships:
They are in readiness.

CAIUS LUCIUS: But what from Rome?

Captain: The senate hath stirr'd up the confiners
And gentlemen of Italy, most willing spirits,
That promise noble service: and they come
Under the conduct of bold Iachimo,
Syenna's brother.

CAIUS LUCIUS: When expect you them?

Captain: With the next benefit o' the wind.

CAIUS LUCIUS: This forwardness
Makes our hopes fair. Command our present numbers
Be muster'd; bid the captains look to't. Now, sir,
What have you dream'd of late of this war's purpose?

Soothsayer: Last night the very gods show'd me a vision--
I fast and pray'd for their intelligence--thus:
I saw Jove's bird, the Roman eagle, wing'd
From the spongy south to this part of the west,
There vanish'd in the sunbeams: which portends--
Unless my sins abuse my divination--
Success to the Roman host.

CAIUS LUCIUS: Dream often so,
And never false. Soft, ho! what trunk is here
Without his top? The ruin speaks that sometime
It was a worthy building. How! a page!
Or dead, or sleeping on him? But dead rather;
For nature doth abhor to make his bed
With the defunct, or sleep upon the dead.
Let's see the boy's face.

Captain: He's alive, my lord.

CAIUS LUCIUS: He'll then instruct us of this body. Young one,

Inform us of thy fortunes, for it seems
They crave to be demanded. Who is this
Thou makest thy bloody pillow? Or who was he
That, otherwise than noble nature did,
Hath alter'd that good picture? What's thy interest
In this sad wreck? How came it? Who is it?
What art thou?

IMOGEN: I am nothing: or if not,
Nothing to be were better. This was my master,
A very valiant Briton and a good,
That here by mountaineers lies slain. Alas!
There is no more such masters: I may wander
From east to occident, cry out for service,
Try many, all good, serve truly, never
Find such another master.

CAIUS LUCIUS: 'Lack, good youth!
Thou movest no less with thy complaining than
Thy master in bleeding: say his name, good friend.

IMOGEN: Richard du Champ.

Aside

If I do lie and do
No harm by it, though the gods hear, I hope
They'll pardon it.--Say you, sir?

CAIUS LUCIUS: Thy name?

IMOGEN: Fidele, sir.

CAIUS LUCIUS: Thou dost approve thyself the very same:
Thy name well fits thy faith, thy faith thy name.
Wilt take thy chance with me? I will not say
Thou shalt be so well master'd, but, be sure,
No less beloved. The Roman emperor's letters,
Sent by a consul to me, should not sooner
Than thine own worth prefer thee: go with me.

IMOGEN: I'll follow, sir. But first, an't please the gods,
I'll hide my master from the flies, as deep
As these poor pickaxes can dig; and when
With wild wood-leaves and weeds I ha' strew'd his grave,
And on it said a century of prayers,
Such as I can, twice o'er, I'll weep and sigh;
And leaving so his service, follow you,
So please you entertain me.

CAIUS LUCIUS: Ay, good youth!
And rather father thee than master thee.
My friends,
The boy hath taught us manly duties: let us
Find out the prettiest daisied plot we can,
And make him with our pikes and partisans
A grave: come, arm him. Boy, he is preferr'd
By thee to us, and he shall be interr'd
As soldiers can. Be cheerful; wipe thine eyes
Some falls are means the happier to arise.

Exeunt

SCENE III. A room in Cymbeline's palace.

Enter CYMBELINE, Lords, PISANIO, and Attendants

CYMBELINE: Again; and bring me word how 'tis with her.

Exit an Attendant

A fever with the absence of her son,
A madness, of which her life's in danger. Heavens,
How deeply you at once do touch me! Imogen,
The great part of my comfort, gone; my queen
Upon a desperate bed, and in a time
When fearful wars point at me; her son gone,
So needful for this present: it strikes me, past
The hope of comfort. But for thee, fellow,
Who needs must know of her departure and
Dost seem so ignorant, we'll enforce it from thee
By a sharp torture.

PISANIO: Sir, my life is yours;
I humbly set it at your will; but, for my mistress,
I nothing know where she remains, why gone,
Nor when she purposes return. Beseech your highness,
Hold me your loyal servant.

First Lord: Good my liege,
The day that she was missing he was here:
I dare be bound he's true and shall perform
All parts of his subjection loyally. For Cloten,
There wants no diligence in seeking him,
And will, no doubt, be found.

CYMBELINE: The time is troublesome.

To PISANIO: We'll slip you for a season; but our jealousy
Does yet depend.

First Lord: So please your majesty,
The Roman legions, all from Gallia drawn,
Are landed on your coast, with a supply
Of Roman gentlemen, by the senate sent.

CYMBELINE: Now for the counsel of my son and queen!
I am amazed with matter.

First Lord: Good my liege,
Your preparation can affront no less
Than what you hear of: come more, for more
you're ready:
The want is but to put those powers in motion
That long to move.

CYMBELINE: I thank you. Let's withdraw;
And meet the time as it seeks us. We fear not
What can from Italy annoy us; but

We grieve at chances here. Away!

Exeunt all but PISANIO

PISANIO: I heard no letter from my master since
I wrote him Imogen was slain: 'tis strange:
Nor hear I from my mistress who did promise
To yield me often tidings: neither know I
What is betid to Cloten; but remain
Perplex'd in all. The heavens still must work.
Wherein I am false I am honest; not true, to be true.
These present wars shall find I love my country,
Even to the note o' the king, or I'll fall in them.
All other doubts, by time let them be clear'd:
Fortune brings in some boats that are not steer'd.

Exit

SCENE IV. Wales: before the cave of Belarius.

Enter BELARIUS, GUIDERIUS, and ARVIRAGUS.

GUIDERIUS: The noise is round about us.

BELARIUS: Let us from it.

ARVIRAGUS: What pleasure, sir, find we in life, to lock it
From action and adventure?

GUIDERIUS: Nay, what hope
Have we in hiding us? This way, the Romans
Must or for Britons slay us, or receive us
For barbarous and unnatural revolts
During their use, and slay us after.

BELARIUS: Sons, We'll higher to the mountains; there secure
us. To the king's party there's no going: newness
Of Cloten's death--we being not known, not muster'd
Among the bands--may drive us to a render
Where we have lived, and so extort from's that
Which we have done, whose answer would be death
Drawn on with torture.

GUIDERIUS: This is, sir, a doubt
In such a time nothing becoming you,
Nor satisfying us.

ARVIRAGUS: It is not likely
That when they hear the Roman horses neigh,
Behold their quarter'd fires, have both their eyes
And ears so cloy'd importantly as now,
That they will waste their time upon our note,
To know from whence we are.

BELARIUS: O, I am known
Of many in the army: many years,
Though Cloten then but young, you see, not wore him
From my remembrance. And, besides, the king
Hath not deserved my service nor your loves;

Who find in my exile the want of breeding,
The certainty of this hard life; aye hopeless
To have the courtesy your cradle promised,
But to be still hot summer's tamings and
The shrinking slaves of winter.

GUIDERIUS: Than be so
Better to cease to be. Pray, sir, to the army:
I and my brother are not known; yourself
So out of thought, and thereto so o'ergrown,
Cannot be question'd.

ARVIRAGUS: By this sun that shines,
I'll thither: what thing is it that I never
Did see man die! scarce ever look'd on blood,
But that of coward hares, hot goats, and venison!
Never bestrid a horse, save one that had
A rider like myself, who ne'er wore rowel
Nor iron on his heel! I am ashamed
To look upon the holy sun, to have
The benefit of his blest beams, remaining
So long a poor unknown.

GUIDERIUS: By heavens, I'll go:
If you will bless me, sir, and give me leave,
I'll take the better care, but if you will not,
The hazard therefore due fall on me by
The hands of Romans!

ARVIRAGUS: So say I amen.

BELARIUS: No reason I, since of your lives you set
So slight a valuation, should reserve
My crack'd one to more care. Have with you, boys!
If in your country wars you chance to die,
That is my bed too, lads, an there I'll lie:
Lead, lead.

Aside

The time seems long; their blood
thinks scorn,
Till it fly out and show them princes born.

Exeunt

ACT V. SCENE I. Britain. The Roman camp.

Enter POSTHUMUS, with a bloody handkerchief

POSTHUMUS LEONATUS: Yea, bloody cloth, I'll keep thee,
for I wish'd Thou shouldst be colour'd thus. You married ones,
If each of you should take this course, how many
Must murder wives much better than themselves
For wrying but a little! O PISANIO!
Every good servant does not all commands:
No bond but to do just ones. Gods! if you
Should have ta'en vengeance on my faults, I never
Had lived to put on this: so had you saved

The noble Imogen to repent, and struck
Me, wretch more worth your vengeance. But, alack,
You snatch some hence for little faults; that's love,
To have them fall no more: you some permit
To second ills with ills, each elder worse,
And make them dread it, to the doers' thrift.
But Imogen is your own: do your best wills,
And make me blest to obey! I am brought hither
Among the Italian gentry, and to fight
Against my lady's kingdom: 'tis enough
That, Britain, I have kill'd thy mistress; peace!
I'll give no wound to thee. Therefore, good heavens,
Hear patiently my purpose: I'll disrobe me
Of these Italian weeds and suit myself
As does a Briton peasant: so I'll fight
Against the part I come with; so I'll die
For thee, O Imogen, even for whom my life
Is every breath a death; and thus, unknown,
Pitied nor hated, to the face of peril
Myself I'll dedicate. Let me make men know
More valour in me than my habits show.
Gods, put the strength o' the Leonati in me!
To shame the guise o' the world, I will begin
The fashion, less without and more within.

Exit

SCENE II. Field of battle between the British and Roman camps.

Enter, from one side, LUCIUS, IACHIMO, and the Roman Army: from the other side, the British Army; POSTHUMUS LEONATUS following, like a poor soldier. They march over and go out. Then enter again, in skirmish, IACHIMO and POSTHUMUS LEONATUS he vanquisheth and disarmeth IACHIMO, and then leaves him

IACHIMO: The heaviness and guilt within my bosom
Takes off my manhood: I have belied a lady,
The princess of this country, and the air on't
Revengingly enfeebles me; or could this carl,
A very drudge of nature's, have subdued me
In my profession? Knighthoods and honours, borne
As I wear mine, are titles but of scorn.
If that thy gentry, Britain, go before
This lout as he exceeds our lords, the odds
Is that we scarce are men and you are gods.

Exit

The battle continues; the Britons fly; CYMBELINE is taken: then enter, to his rescue, BELARIUS, GUIDERIUS, and ARVIRAGUS

BELARIUS: Stand, stand! We have the advantage of the ground; The lane is guarded: nothing routs us but
The villany of our fears.

GUIDERIUS ARVIRAGUS: Stand, stand, and fight!

Re-enter POSTHUMUS LEONATUS, and seconds the Britons: they rescue CYMBELINE, and exeunt. Then re-enter LUCIUS, and IACHIMO, with IMOGEN

CAIUS LUCIUS: Away, boy, from the troops, and save thyself;
For friends kill friends, and the disorder's such
As war were hoodwink'd.

IACHIMO: 'Tis their fresh supplies.

CAIUS LUCIUS: It is a day turn'd strangely: or betimes
Let's reinforce, or fly.

Exeunt

SCENE III. Another part of the field.

Enter POSTHUMUS LEONATUS and a British Lord

Lord: Camest thou from where they made the stand?

POSTHUMUS LEONATUS: I did.
Though you, it seems, come from the fliers.

Lord: I did.

POSTHUMUS LEONATUS: No blame be to you, sir; for all was lost, But that the heavens fought: the king himself
Of his wings destitute, the army broken,
And but the backs of Britons seen, all flying
Through a straight lane; the enemy full-hearted,
Lolling the tongue with slaughtering, having work
More plentiful than tools to do't, struck down
Some mortally, some slightly touch'd, some falling
Merely through fear; that the straight pass was damm'd
With dead men hurt behind, and cowards living
To die with lengthen'd shame.

Lord: Where was this lane?

POSTHUMUS LEONATUS: Close by the battle, ditch'd, and wall'd with turf; Which gave advantage to an ancient soldier,
An honest one, I warrant; who deserved
So long a breeding as his white beard came to,
In doing this for's country: athwart the lane,
He, with two striplings-lads more like to run
The country base than to commit such slaughter
With faces fit for masks, or rather fairer
Than those for preservation cased, or shame--
Made good the passage; cried to those that fled,
'Our Britain s harts die flying, not our men:
To darkness fleet souls that fly backwards. Stand;
Or we are Romans and will give you that
Like beasts which you shun beastly, and may save,
But to look back in frown: stand, stand.'
These three,

Three thousand confident, in act as many--
For three performers are the file when all
The rest do nothing--with this word 'Stand, stand,'
Accommodated by the place, more charming
With their own nobleness, which could have turn'd
A distaff to a lance, gilded pale looks,
Part shame, part spirit renew'd; that some,
turn'd coward
But by example--O, a sin in war,
Damn'd in the first beginners!--gan to look
The way that they did, and to grin like lions
Upon the pikes o' the hunters. Then began
A stop i' the chaser, a retire, anon
A rout, confusion thick; forthwith they fly
Chickens, the way which they stoop'd eagles; slaves,
The strides they victors made: and now our cowards,
Like fragments in hard voyages, became
The life o' the need: having found the backdoor open
Of the unguarded hearts, heavens, how they wound!
Some slain before; some dying; some their friends
O'er borne i' the former wave: ten, chased by one,
Are now each one the slaughter-man of twenty:
Those that would die or ere resist are grown
The mortal bugs o' the field.

Lord: This was strange chance
A narrow lane, an old man, and two boys.

POSTHUMUS LEONATUS: Nay, do not wonder at it: you are made Rather to wonder at the things you hear

Than to work any. Will you rhyme upon't,
And vent it for a mockery? Here is one:
'Two boys, an old man twice a boy, a lane,
Preserved the Britons, was the Romans' bane.'

Lord: Nay, be not angry, sir.

POSTHUMUS LEONATUS: 'Lack, to what end?
Who dares not stand his foe, I'll be his friend;
For if he'll do as he is made to do,
I know he'll quickly fly my friendship too.
You have put me into rhyme.

Lord: Farewell; you're angry.

POSTHUMUS LEONATUS: Still going?

Exit Lord

This is a lord! O noble misery,
To be i' the field, and ask 'what news?' of me!
To-day how many would have given their honours
To have saved their carcasses! took heel to do't,
And yet died too! I, in mine own woe charm'd,
Could not find death where I did hear him groan,
Nor feel him where he struck: being an ugly monster,
'Tis strange he hides him in fresh cups, soft beds,
Sweet words; or hath more ministers than we
That draw his knives i' the war. Well, I will find him
For being now a favourer to the Briton,

No more a Briton, I have resumed again
The part I came in: fight I will no more,
But yield me to the veriest hind that shall
Once touch my shoulder. Great the slaughter is
Here made by the Roman; great the answer be
Britons must take. For me, my ransom's death;
On either side I come to spend my breath;
Which neither here I'll keep nor bear again,
But end it by some means for Imogen.

Enter two British Captains and Soldiers

First Captain: Great Jupiter be praised! Lucius is taken.
'Tis thought the old man and his sons were angels.
Second Captain: There was a fourth man, in a silly habit,
That gave the affront with them.
First Captain: So 'tis reported:
But none of 'em can be found. Stand! who's there?

POSTHUMUS LEONATUS: A Roman,
Who had not now been drooping here, if seconds
Had answer'd him.

Second Captain: Lay hands on him; a dog!
A leg of Rome shall not return to tell
What crows have peck'd them here. He brags
his service As if he were of note: bring him to the king.

Enter CYMBELINE, BELARIUS, GUIDERIUS, ARVIRAGUS,

PISANIO: , Soldiers, Attendants, and Roman Captives. The Captains present POSTHUMUS LEONATUS to CYMBELINE, who delivers him over to a Gaoler:
Then exeunt Omnes

SCENE IV. A British prison.

Enter POSTHUMUS LEONATUS and two Gaolers

First Gaoler: You shall not now be stol'n, you have locks upon you; So graze as you find pasture.

Second Gaoler: Ay, or a stomach.

Exeunt Gaolers

POSTHUMUS LEONATUS: Most welcome, bondage! for thou art away, think, to liberty: yet am I better
Than one that's sick o' the gout; since he had rather
Groan so in perpetuity than be cured
By the sure physician, death, who is the key
To unbar these locks. My conscience, thou art fetter'd
More than my shanks and wrists: you good gods, give me
The penitent instrument to pick that bolt,
Then, free for ever! Is't enough I am sorry?
So children temporal fathers do appease;
Gods are more full of mercy. Must I repent?
I cannot do it better than in gyves,
Desired more than constrain'd: to satisfy,

If of my freedom 'tis the main part, take
No stricter render of me than my all.
I know you are more clement than vile men,
Who of their broken debtors take a third,
A sixth, a tenth, letting them thrive again
On their abatement: that's not my desire:
For Imogen's dear life take mine; and though
'Tis not so dear, yet 'tis a life; you coin'd it:
'Tween man and man they weigh not every stamp;
Though light, take pieces for the figure's sake:
You rather mine, being yours: and so, great powers,
If you will take this audit, take this life,
And cancel these cold bonds. O Imogen!
I'll speak to thee in silence.

Sleeps

Solemn music.

Enter, as in an apparition, SICILIUS LEONATUS, father to Posthumus Leonatus, an old man, attired like a warrior; leading in his hand an ancient matron, his wife, and mother to Posthumus Leonatus, with music before them: then, after other music, follow the two young Leonati, brothers to Posthumus Leonatus, with wounds as they died in the wars. They circle Posthumus Leonatus round, as he lies sleeping

Sicilius Leonatus: No more, thou thunder-master, show
Thy spite on mortal flies:
With Mars fall out, with Juno chide,

That thy adulteries
Rates and revenges.
Hath my poor boy done aught but well,
Whose face I never saw?
I died whilst in the womb he stay'd
Attending nature's law:
Whose father then, as men report
Thou orphans' father art,
Thou shouldst have been, and shielded him
From this earth-vexing smart.

Mother: Lucina lent not me her aid,
But took me in my throes;
That from me was Posthumus ript,
Came crying 'mongst his foes,
A thing of pity!

Sicilius Leonatus: Great nature, like his ancestry,
Moulded the stuff so fair,
That he deserved the praise o' the world,
As great Sicilius' heir.

First Brother: When once he was mature for man,
In Britain where was he
That could stand up his parallel;
Or fruitful object be
In eye of Imogen, that best
Could deem his dignity?

Mother: With marriage wherefore was he mock'd,

To be exiled, and thrown
From Leonati seat, and cast
From her his dearest one,
Sweet Imogen?

Sicilius Leonatus: Why did you suffer Iachimo,
Slight thing of Italy,
To taint his nobler heart and brain
With needless jealosy;
And to become the geck and scorn
O' th' other's villany?

Second Brother: For this from stiller seats we came,
Our parents and us twain,
That striking in our country's cause
Fell bravely and were slain,
Our fealty and Tenantius' right
With honour to maintain.

First Brother: Like hardiment Posthumus hath
To Cymbeline perform'd:
Then, Jupiter, thou king of gods,
Why hast thou thus adjourn'd
The graces for his merits due,
Being all to dolours turn'd?

Sicilius Leonatus: Thy crystal window ope; look out;
No longer exercise
Upon a valiant race thy harsh
And potent injuries.

Mother: Since, Jupiter, our son is good,
Take off his miseries.

Sicilius Leonatus: Peep through thy marble mansion; help;
Or we poor ghosts will cry
To the shining synod of the rest
Against thy deity.

First Brother Second Brother: Help, Jupiter; or we appeal,
And from thy justice fly.

Jupiter descends in thunder and lightning, sitting upon an eagle: he throws a thunderbolt. The Apparitions fall on their knees

Jupiter: No more, you petty spirits of region low,
Offend our hearing; hush! How dare you ghosts
Accuse the thunderer, whose bolt, you know,
Sky-planted batters all rebelling coasts?
Poor shadows of Elysium, hence, and rest
Upon your never-withering banks of flowers:
Be not with mortal accidents opprest;
No care of yours it is; you know 'tis ours.
Whom best I love I cross; to make my gift,
The more delay'd, delighted. Be content;
Your low-laid son our godhead will uplift:
His comforts thrive, his trials well are spent.
Our Jovial star reign'd at his birth, and in
Our temple was he married. Rise, and fade.

He shall be lord of lady Imogen,
And happier much by his affliction made.
This tablet lay upon his breast, wherein
Our pleasure his full fortune doth confine:
and so, away: no further with your din
Express impatience, lest you stir up mine.
Mount, eagle, to my palace crystalline.

Ascends

Sicilius Leonatus: He came in thunder; his celestial breath
Was sulphurous to smell: the holy eagle
Stoop'd as to foot us: his ascension is
More sweet than our blest fields: his royal bird
Prunes the immortal wing and cloys his beak,
As when his god is pleased.

All: Thanks, Jupiter!

Sicilius Leonatus: The marble pavement closes, he is enter'd
His radiant root. Away! and, to be blest,
Let us with care perform his great behest.

The Apparitions vanish

POSTHUMUS LEONATUS: [Waking] Sleep, thou hast been a grandsire, and begot
A father to me; and thou hast created
A mother and two brothers: but, O scorn!
Gone! they went hence so soon as they were born:

And so I am awake. Poor wretches that depend
On greatness' favour dream as I have done,
Wake and find nothing. But, alas, I swerve:
Many dream not to find, neither deserve,
And yet are steep'd in favours: so am I,
That have this golden chance and know not why.
What fairies haunt this ground? A book? O rare one!
Be not, as is our fangled world, a garment
Nobler than that it covers: let thy effects
So follow, to be most unlike our courtiers,
As good as promise.

Reads

'When as a lion's whelp shall, to himself unknown, without seeking find, and be embraced by a piece of tender air; and when from a stately cedar shall be lopped branches, which, being dead many years, shall after revive, be jointed to the old stock and freshly grow; then shall Posthumus end his miseries, Britain be fortunate and flourish in peace and plenty.'
'Tis still a dream, or else such stuff as madmen
Tongue and brain not; either both or nothing;
Or senseless speaking or a speaking such
As sense cannot untie. Be what it is,
The action of my life is like it, which
I'll keep, if but for sympathy.

Re-enter First Gaoler

First Gaoler: Come, sir, are you ready for death?

POSTHUMUS LEONATUS: Over-roasted rather; ready long ago.

First Gaoler: Hanging is the word, sir: if
you be ready for that, you are well cooked.

POSTHUMUS LEONATUS: So, if I prove a good repast to the spectators, the dish pays the shot.

First Gaoler: A heavy reckoning for you, sir. But the comfort is,
you shall be called to no more payments, fear no
more tavern-bills; which are often the sadness of
parting, as the procuring of mirth: you come in
flint for want of meat, depart reeling with too
much drink; sorry that you have paid too much, and
sorry that you are paid too much; purse and brain
both empty; the brain the heavier for being too
light, the purse too light, being drawn of
heaviness: of this contradiction you shall now be
quit. O, the charity of a penny cord! It sums up
thousands in a trice: you have no true debitor and
creditor but it; of what's past, is, and to come,
the discharge: your neck, sir, is pen, book and
counters; so the acquittance follows.

POSTHUMUS LEONATUS: I am merrier to die than thou art to live.

First Gaoler: Indeed, sir, he that sleeps feels not the tooth-ache: but a man that were to sleep your sleep, and a hangman to help him to bed, I think he would change places with his officer; for, look you, sir, you know not which way you shall go.

POSTHUMUS LEONATUS: Yes, indeed do I, fellow.

First Gaoler: Your death has eyes in 's head then; I have not seen him so pictured: you must either be directed by some that take upon them to know, or do take upon yourself that which I am sure you do not know, or jump the after inquiry on your own peril: and how you shall speed in your journey's end, I think you'll never return to tell one.

POSTHUMUS LEONATUS: I tell thee, fellow, there are none want eyes to direct them the way I am going, but such as wink and will not use them.

First Gaoler: What an infinite mock is this, that a man should have the best use of eyes to see the way of blindness! I am sure hanging's the way of winking.

Enter a Messenger

Messenger: Knock off his manacles; bring your prisoner to the king.

POSTHUMUS LEONATUS: Thou bring'st good news; I am called to be made free.

First Gaoler: I'll be hang'd then.

POSTHUMUS LEONATUS: Thou shalt be then freer than a gaoler; no bolts for the dead.

Exeunt POSTHUMUS LEONATUS and Messenger

First Gaoler: Unless a man would marry a gallows and beget young gibbets, I never saw one so prone. Yet, on my conscience, there are verier knaves desire to live, for all he be a Roman: and there be some of them too that die against their wills; so should I, if I were one. I would we were all of one mind, and one mind good; O, there were desolation of gaolers and gallowses! I speak against my present profit, but my wish hath a preferment in 't.

Exeunt

SCENE V. Cymbeline's tent.

Enter CYMBELINE, BELARIUS, GUIDERIUS, ARVIRAGUS, PISANIO, Lords, Officers, and Attendants

CYMBELINE: Stand by my side, you whom the gods have made Preservers of my throne. Woe is my heart

That the poor soldier that so richly fought,
Whose rags shamed gilded arms, whose naked breast
Stepp'd before larges of proof, cannot be found:
He shall be happy that can find him, if
Our grace can make him so.

BELARIUS: I never saw
Such noble fury in so poor a thing;
Such precious deeds in one that promises nought
But beggary and poor looks.

CYMBELINE: No tidings of him?

PISANIO: He hath been search'd among the dead and living,
But no trace of him.

CYMBELINE: To my grief, I am
The heir of his reward;

To BELARIUS, GUIDERIUS, and ARVIRAGUS: which I will
add To you, the liver, heart and brain of Britain,
By whom I grant she lives. 'Tis now the time
To ask of whence you are. Report it.

BELARIUS: Sir, In Cambria are we born, and gentlemen:
Further to boast were neither true nor modest,
Unless I add, we are honest.

CYMBELINE: Bow your knees.
Arise my knights o' the battle: I create you

Companions to our person and will fit you
With dignities becoming your estates.

Enter CORNELIUS and Ladies

There's business in these faces. Why so sadly
Greet you our victory? you look like Romans,
And not o' the court of Britain.

CORNELIUS: Hail, great king!
To sour your happiness, I must report
The queen is dead.

CYMBELINE: Who worse than a physician
Would this report become? But I consider,
By medicine life may be prolong'd, yet death
Will seize the doctor too. How ended she?

CORNELIUS: With horror, madly dying, like her life,
Which, being cruel to the world, concluded
Most cruel to herself. What she confess'd
I will report, so please you: these her women
Can trip me, if I err; who with wet cheeks
Were present when she finish'd.

CYMBELINE: Prithee, say.

CORNELIUS: First, she confess'd she never loved you, only
Affected greatness got by you, not you:
Married your royalty, was wife to your place;

Abhorr'd your person.

CYMBELINE: She alone knew this;
And, but she spoke it dying, I would not
Believe her lips in opening it. Proceed.

CORNELIUS: Your daughter, whom she bore in hand to love
With such integrity, she did confess
Was as a scorpion to her sight; whose life,
But that her flight prevented it, she had
Ta'en off by poison.

CYMBELINE: O most delicate fiend!
Who is 't can read a woman? Is there more?

CORNELIUS: More, sir, and worse. She did confess she had
For you a mortal mineral; which, being took,
Should by the minute feed on life and lingering
By inches waste you: in which time she purposed,
By watching, weeping, tendance, kissing, to
O'ercome you with her show, and in time,
When she had fitted you with her craft, to work
Her son into the adoption of the crown:
But, failing of her end by his strange absence,
Grew shameless-desperate; open'd, in despite
Of heaven and men, her purposes; repented
The evils she hatch'd were not effected; so
Despairing died.

CYMBELINE: Heard you all this, her women?

First Lady: We did, so please your highness.

CYMBELINE: Mine eyes
Were not in fault, for she was beautiful;
Mine ears, that heard her flattery; nor my heart,
That thought her like her seeming; it had
been vicious To have mistrusted her: yet, O my daughter!
That it was folly in me, thou mayst say,
And prove it in thy feeling. Heaven mend all!

Enter LUCIUS, IACHIMO, the Soothsayer, and other Roman Prisoners, guarded; POSTHUMUS LEONATUS behind, and IMOGEN

Thou comest not, Caius, now for tribute that
The Britons have razed out, though with the loss
Of many a bold one; whose kinsmen have made suit
That their good souls may be appeased with slaughter
Of you their captives, which ourself have granted:
So think of your estate.

CAIUS LUCIUS: Consider, sir, the chance of war: the day
Was yours by accident; had it gone with us,
We should not, when the blood was cool,
have threaten'd Our prisoners with the sword. But since the
gods Will have it thus, that nothing but our lives
May be call'd ransom, let it come: sufficeth
A Roman with a Roman's heart can suffer:
Augustus lives to think on't: and so much

For my peculiar care. This one thing only
I will entreat; my boy, a Briton born,
Let him be ransom'd: never master had
A page so kind, so duteous, diligent,
So tender over his occasions, true,
So feat, so nurse-like: let his virtue join
With my request, which I make bold your highness
Cannot deny; he hath done no Briton harm,
Though he have served a Roman: save him, sir,
And spare no blood beside.

CYMBELINE: I have surely seen him:
His favour is familiar to me. Boy,
Thou hast look'd thyself into my grace,
And art mine own. I know not why, wherefore,
To say 'live, boy:' ne'er thank thy master; live:
And ask of Cymbeline what boon thou wilt,
Fitting my bounty and thy state, I'll give it;
Yea, though thou do demand a prisoner,
The noblest ta'en.

IMOGEN: I humbly thank your highness.

CAIUS LUCIUS: I do not bid thee beg my life, good lad;
And yet I know thou wilt.

IMOGEN: No, no: alack,
There's other work in hand: I see a thing
Bitter to me as death: your life, good master,
Must shuffle for itself.

CAIUS LUCIUS: The boy disdains me,
He leaves me, scorns me: briefly die their joys
That place them on the truth of girls and boys.
Why stands he so perplex'd?

CYMBELINE: What wouldst thou, boy?
I love thee more and more: think more and more
What's best to ask. Know'st him thou look'st on? speak,
Wilt have him live? Is he thy kin? thy friend?

IMOGEN: He is a Roman; no more kin to me
Than I to your highness; who, being born your vassal,
Am something nearer.

CYMBELINE: Wherefore eyest him so?

IMOGEN: I'll tell you, sir, in private, if you please
To give me hearing.

CYMBELINE: Ay, with all my heart,
And lend my best attention. What's thy name?

IMOGEN: Fidele, sir.

CYMBELINE: Thou'rt my good youth, my page;
I'll be thy master: walk with me; speak freely.

CYMBELINE and IMOGEN converse apart

BELARIUS: Is not this boy revived from death?

ARVIRAGUS: One sand another
Not more resembles that sweet rosy lad
Who died, and was Fidele. What think you?

GUIDERIUS: The same dead thing alive.

BELARIUS: Peace, peace! see further; he eyes us not;
forbear; Creatures may be alike: were 't he, I am sure
He would have spoke to us.

GUIDERIUS: But we saw him dead.

BELARIUS: Be silent; let's see further.

PISANIO: *[Aside]* It is my mistress:
Since she is living, let the time run on
To good or bad.

CYMBELINE and IMOGEN come forward

CYMBELINE: Come, stand thou by our side;
Make thy demand aloud.

To IACHIMO: Sir, step you forth;
Give answer to this boy, and do it freely;
Or, by our greatness and the grace of it,
Which is our honour, bitter torture shall
Winnow the truth from falsehood. On, speak to him.

IMOGEN: My boon is, that this gentleman may render
Of whom he had this ring.

POSTHUMUS LEONATUS: *[Aside]* What's that to him?

CYMBELINE: That diamond upon your finger, say
How came it yours?

IACHIMO: Thou'lt torture me to leave unspoken that
Which, to be spoke, would torture thee.

CYMBELINE: How! me?

IACHIMO: I am glad to be constrain'd to utter that
Which torments me to conceal. By villany
I got this ring: 'twas Leonatus' jewel;
Whom thou didst banish; and--which more may
grieve thee, As it doth me--a nobler sir ne'er lived
'Twixt sky and ground. Wilt thou hear more, my lord?

CYMBELINE: All that belongs to this.

IACHIMO: That paragon, thy daughter,--
For whom my heart drops blood, and my false spirits
Quail to remember--Give me leave; I faint.

CYMBELINE: My daughter! what of her? Renew thy strength:
I had rather thou shouldst live while nature will
Than die ere I hear more: strive, man, and speak.

IACHIMO: Upon a time,--unhappy was the clock
That struck the hour!--it was in Rome,--accursed
The mansion where!--'twas at a feast,--O, would
Our viands had been poison'd, or at least
Those which I heaved to head!--the good Posthumus--
What should I say? he was too good to be
Where ill men were; and was the best of all
Amongst the rarest of good ones,--sitting sadly,
Hearing us praise our loves of Italy
For beauty that made barren the swell'd boast
Of him that best could speak, for feature, laming
The shrine of Venus, or straight-pight Minerva.
Postures beyond brief nature, for condition,
A shop of all the qualities that man
Loves woman for, besides that hook of wiving,
Fairness which strikes the eye--

CYMBELINE: I stand on fire: Come to the matter.

IACHIMO: All too soon I shall,
Unless thou wouldst grieve quickly. This Posthumus,
Most like a noble lord in love and one
That had a royal lover, took his hint;
And, not dispraising whom we praised,--therein
He was as calm as virtue--he began
His mistress' picture; which by his tongue
being made,
And then a mind put in't, either our brags
Were crack'd of kitchen-trolls, or his description

Proved us unspeaking sots.

CYMBELINE: Nay, nay, to the purpose.

IACHIMO: Your daughter's chastity--there it begins.
He spake of her, as Dian had hot dreams,
And she alone were cold: whereat I, wretch,
Made scruple of his praise; and wager'd with him
Pieces of gold 'gainst this which then he wore
Upon his honour'd finger, to attain
In suit the place of's bed and win this ring
By hers and mine adultery. He, true knight,
No lesser of her honour confident
Than I did truly find her, stakes this ring;
And would so, had it been a carbuncle
Of Phoebus' wheel, and might so safely, had it
Been all the worth of's car. Away to Britain
Post I in this design: well may you, sir,
Remember me at court; where I was taught
Of your chaste daughter the wide difference
'Twixt amorous and villanous. Being thus quench'd
Of hope, not longing, mine Italian brain
'Gan in your duller Britain operate
Most vilely; for my vantage, excellent:
And, to be brief, my practise so prevail'd,
That I return'd with simular proof enough
To make the noble Leonatus mad,
By wounding his belief in her renown
With tokens thus, and thus; averting notes
Of chamber-hanging, pictures, this her bracelet,--

O cunning, how I got it!--nay, some marks
Of secret on her person, that he could not
But think her bond of chastity quite crack'd,
I having ta'en the forfeit. Whereupon--
Methinks, I see him now--

POSTHUMUS LEONATUS: *[Advancing]* Ay, so thou dost,
Italian fiend! Ay me, most credulous fool,
Egregious murderer, thief, any thing
That's due to all the villains past, in being,
To come! O, give me cord, or knife, or poison,
Some upright justicer! Thou, king, send out
For torturers ingenious: it is I
That all the abhorred things o' the earth amend
By being worse than they. I am Posthumus,
That kill'd thy daughter:--villain-like, I lie--
That caused a lesser villain than myself,
A sacrilegious thief, to do't: the temple
Of virtue was she; yea, and she herself.
Spit, and throw stone s, cast mire upon me, set
The dogs o' the street to bay me: every villain
Be call'd Posthumus Leonitus; and
Be villany less than 'twas! O Imogen!
My queen, my life, my wife! O Imogen,
Imogen, Imogen!

IMOGEN: Peace, my lord; hear, hear--

POSTHUMUS LEONATUS: Shall's have a play of this? Thou scornful page,

There lie thy part.

Striking her: she falls

PISANIO: O, gentlemen, help!
Mine and your mistress! O, my lord Posthumus!
You ne'er kill'd Imogen til now. Help, help!
Mine honour'd lady!

CYMBELINE: Does the world go round?

POSTHUMUS LEONATUS: How come these staggers on me?

PISANIO: Wake, my mistress!

CYMBELINE: If this be so, the gods do mean to strike me
To death with mortal joy.

PISANIO: How fares thy mistress?

IMOGEN: O, get thee from my sight;
Thou gavest me poison: dangerous fellow, hence!
Breathe not where princes are.

CYMBELINE: The tune of Imogen!

PISANIO: Lady,
The gods throw stones of sulphur on me, if
That box I gave you was not thought by me

A precious thing: I had it from the queen.

CYMBELINE: New matter still?

IMOGEN: It poison'd me.

CORNELIUS: O gods! I left out one thing which the queen
confess'd. Which must approve thee honest: 'If PISANIO
Have,' said she, 'given his mistress that confection
Which I gave him for cordial, she is served
As I would serve a rat.'

CYMBELINE: What's this, Comelius?

CORNELIUS: The queen, sir, very oft importuned me
To temper poisons for her, still pretending
The satisfaction of her knowledge only
In killing creatures vile, as cats and dogs,
Of no esteem: I, dreading that her purpose
Was of more danger, did compound for her
A certain stuff, which, being ta'en, would cease
The present power of life, but in short time
All offices of nature should again
Do their due functions. Have you ta'en of it?

IMOGEN: Most like I did, for I was dead.

BELARIUS: My boys, There was our error.

GUIDERIUS: This is, sure, Fidele.

IMOGEN: Why did you throw your wedded lady from you?
Think that you are upon a rock; and now
Throw me again.

Embracing him

POSTHUMUS LEONATUS: Hang there like a fruit, my soul,
Till the tree die!

CYMBELINE: How now, my flesh, my child!
What, makest thou me a dullard in this act?
Wilt thou not speak to me?

IMOGEN: *[Kneeling]* Your blessing, sir.

BELARIUS: *[To GUIDERIUS and ARVIRAGUS]* Though you did love this youth, I blame ye not:
You had a motive for't.

CYMBELINE: My tears that fall
Prove holy water on thee! Imogen,
Thy mother's dead.

IMOGEN: I am sorry for't, my lord.

CYMBELINE: O, she was nought; and long of her it was
That we meet here so strangely: but her son
Is gone, we know not how nor where.

PISANIO: My lord, Now fear is from me, I'll speak troth. Lord
Cloten, Upon my lady's missing, came to me
With his sword drawn; foam'd at the mouth, and swore,
If I discover'd not which way she was gone,
It was my instant death. By accident,
had a feigned letter of my master's
Then in my pocket; which directed him
To seek her on the mountains near to Milford;
Where, in a frenzy, in my master's garments,
Which he enforced from me, away he posts
With unchaste purpose and with oath to violate
My lady's honour: what became of him
I further know not.

GUIDERIUS: Let me end the story: I slew him there.

CYMBELINE: Marry, the gods forfend!
I would not thy good deeds should from my lips
Pluck a bard sentence: prithee, valiant youth,
Deny't again.

GUIDERIUS: I have spoke it, and I did it.

CYMBELINE: He was a prince.

GUIDERIUS: A most incivil one: the wrongs he did me
Were nothing prince-like; for he did provoke me
With language that would make me spurn the sea,
If it could so roar to me: I cut off's head;
And am right glad he is not standing here

To tell this tale of mine.

CYMBELINE: I am sorry for thee:
By thine own tongue thou art condemn'd, and must
Endure our law: thou'rt dead.

IMOGEN: That headless man I thought had been my lord.

CYMBELINE: Bind the offender, And take him from our presence.

BELARIUS: Stay, sir king:
This man is better than the man he slew,
As well descended as thyself; and hath
More of thee merited than a band of Clotens
Had ever scar for. To the Guard
Let his arms alone; They were not born for bondage.

CYMBELINE: Why, old soldier,
Wilt thou undo the worth thou art unpaid for,
By tasting of our wrath? How of descent
As good as we?

ARVIRAGUS: In that he spake too far.

CYMBELINE: And thou shalt die for't.

BELARIUS: We will die all three:
But I will prove that two on's are as good
As I have given out him. My sons, I must,

For mine own part, unfold a dangerous speech,
Though, haply, well for you.

ARVIRAGUS: Your danger's ours.

GUIDERIUS: And our good his.

BELARIUS: Have at it then, by leave.
Thou hadst, great king, a subject who
Was call'd Belarius.

CYMBELINE: What of him? he is
A banish'd traitor.

BELARIUS: He it is that hath
Assumed this age; indeed a banish'd man;
I know not how a traitor.

CYMBELINE: Take him hence:
The whole world shall not save him.

BELARIUS: Not too hot:
First pay me for the nursing of thy sons;
And let it be confiscate all, so soon
As I have received it.

CYMBELINE: Nursing of my sons!

BELARIUS: I am too blunt and saucy: here's my knee:
Ere I arise, I will prefer my sons;

Then spare not the old father. Mighty sir,
These two young gentlemen, that call me father
And think they are my sons, are none of mine;
They are the issue of your loins, my liege,
And blood of your begetting.

CYMBELINE: How! my issue!

BELARIUS: So sure as you your father's. I, old Morgan,
Am that Belarius whom you sometime banish'd:
Your pleasure was my mere offence, my punishment
Itself, and all my treason; that I suffer'd
Was all the harm I did. These gentle princes--
For such and so they are--these twenty years
Have I train'd up: those arts they have as I
Could put into them; my breeding was, sir, as
Your highness knows. Their nurse, Euriphile,
Whom for the theft I wedded, stole these children
Upon my banishment: I moved her to't,
Having received the punishment before,
For that which I did then: beaten for loyalty
Excited me to treason: their dear loss,
The more of you 'twas felt, the more it shaped
Unto my end of stealing them. But, gracious sir,
Here are your sons again; and I must lose
Two of the sweet'st companions in the world.
The benediction of these covering heavens
Fall on their heads like dew! for they are worthy
To inlay heaven with stars.

CYMBELINE: Thou weep'st, and speak'st.
The service that you three have done is more
Unlike than this thou tell'st. I lost my children:
If these be they, I know not how to wish
A pair of worthier sons.

BELARIUS: Be pleased awhile.
This gentleman, whom I call Polydore,
Most worthy prince, as yours, is true Guiderius:
This gentleman, my Cadwal, Arviragus,
Your younger princely son; he, sir, was lapp'd
In a most curious mantle, wrought by the hand
Of his queen mother, which for more probation
I can with ease produce.

CYMBELINE: Guiderius had
Upon his neck a mole, a sanguine star;
It was a mark of wonder.

BELARIUS: This is he;
Who hath upon him still that natural stamp:
It was wise nature's end in the donation,
To be his evidence now.

CYMBELINE: O, what, am I
A mother to the birth of three? Ne'er mother
Rejoiced deliverance more. Blest pray you be,
That, after this strange starting from your orbs,
may reign in them now! O Imogen,
Thou hast lost by this a kingdom.

IMOGEN: No, my lord; I have got two worlds by 't. O my gentle brothers, Have we thus met? O, never say hereafter
But I am truest speaker you call'd me brother,
When I was but your sister; I you brothers,
When ye were so indeed.

CYMBELINE: Did you e'er meet?

ARVIRAGUS: Ay, my good lord.

GUIDERIUS: And at first meeting loved;
Continued so, until we thought he died.

CORNELIUS: By the queen's dram she swallow'd.

CYMBELINE: O rare instinct!
When shall I hear all through? This fierce
Abridgement Hath to it circumstantial branches, which
Distinction should be rich in. Where? how lived You?
And when came you to serve our Roman captive?
How parted with your brothers? how first met them?
Why fled you from the court? and whither? These,
And your three motives to the battle, with
I know not how much more, should be demanded;
And all the other by-dependencies,
From chance to chance: but nor the time nor place
Will serve our long inter'gatories. See,
Posthumus anchors upon Imogen,
And she, like harmless lightning, throws her eye

On him, her brother, me, her master, hitting
Each object with a joy: the counterchange
Is severally in all. Let's quit this ground,
And smoke the temple with our sacrifices.

To BELARIUS: Thou art my brother; so we'll hold thee ever.

IMOGEN: You are my father too, and did relieve me,
To see this gracious season.

CYMBELINE: All o'erjoy'd,
Save these in bonds: let them be joyful too,
For they shall taste our comfort.

IMOGEN: My good master,
I will yet do you service.

CAIUS LUCIUS: Happy be you!

CYMBELINE: The forlorn soldier, that so nobly fought,
He would have well becomed this place, and graced
The thankings of a king.

POSTHUMUS LEONATUS: I am, sir,
The soldier that did company these three
In poor beseeming; 'twas a fitment for
The purpose I then follow'd. That I was he,
Speak, Iachimo: I had you down and might
Have made you finish.

IACHIMO: *[Kneeling]* I am down again:
But now my heavy conscience sinks my knee,
As then your force did. Take that life, beseech you,
Which I so often owe: but your ring first;
And here the bracelet of the truest princess
That ever swore her faith.

POSTHUMUS LEONATUS: Kneel not to me:
The power that I have on you is, to spare you;
The malice towards you to forgive you: live,
And deal with others better.

CYMBELINE: Nobly doom'd!
We'll learn our freeness of a son-in-law;
Pardon's the word to all.

ARVIRAGUS: You holp us, sir,
As you did mean indeed to be our brother;
Joy'd are we that you are.

POSTHUMUS LEONATUS: Your servant, princes. Good my lord of Rome, Call forth your soothsayer: as I slept, methought
Great Jupiter, upon his eagle back'd,
Appear'd to me, with other spritely shows
Of mine own kindred: when I waked, I found
This label on my bosom; whose containing
Is so from sense in hardness, that I can
Make no collection of it: let him show
His skill in the construction.

CAIUS LUCIUS: Philarmonus!

Soothsayer: Here, my good lord.

CAIUS LUCIUS: Read, and declare the meaning.

Soothsayer: *[Reads]* 'When as a lion's whelp shall, to himself unknown, without seeking find, and be embraced by a piece of tender air; and when from a stately cedar shall be lopped branches, which, being dead many years, shall after revive, be jointed to the old stock, and freshly grow; then shall Posthumus end his miseries, Britain be fortunate and flourish in peace and plenty.'
Thou, Leonatus, art the lion's whelp;
The fit and apt construction of thy name,
Being Leonatus, doth import so much.

To CYMBELINE: The piece of tender air, thy virtuous daughter, Which we call 'mollis aer;' and 'mollis aer' We term it 'mulier:' which 'mulier' I divine
Is this most constant wife; who, even now,
Answering the letter of the oracle,
Unknown to you, unsought, were clipp'd about
With this most tender air.

CYMBELINE: This hath some seeming.

Soothsayer: The lofty cedar, royal Cymbeline,
Personates thee: and thy lopp'd branches point

Thy two sons forth; who, by Belarius stol'n,
For many years thought dead, are now revived,
To the majestic cedar join'd, whose issue
Promises Britain peace and plenty.

CYMBELINE: Well My peace we will begin. And, Caius
Lucius, Although the victor, we submit to Caesar,
And to the Roman empire; promising
To pay our wonted tribute, from the which
We were dissuaded by our wicked queen;
Whom heavens, in justice, both on her and hers,
Have laid most heavy hand.

Soothsayer: The fingers of the powers above do tune
The harmony of this peace. The vision
Which I made known to Lucius, ere the stroke
Of this yet scarce-cold battle, at this instant
Is full accomplish'd; for the Roman eagle,
From south to west on wing soaring aloft,
Lessen'd herself, and in the beams o' the sun
So vanish'd: which foreshow'd our princely eagle,
The imperial Caesar, should again unite
His favour with the radiant Cymbeline,
Which shines here in the west.

CYMBELINE: Laud we the gods;
And let our crooked smokes climb to their nostrils
From our blest altars. Publish we this peace
To all our subjects. Set we forward: let
A Roman and a British ensign wave

Friendly together: so through Lud's-town march:
And in the temple of great Jupiter
Our peace we'll ratify; seal it with feasts.
Set on there! Never was a war did cease,
Ere bloody hands were wash'd, with such a peace.

Exeunt

*** * * Plot of CYMBELINE per Wikipedia* * ***

Cymbeline /ˈsɪmbɪliːn/, also known as Cymbeline, King of Britain, is a play by William Shakespeare set in Ancient Britain and based on legends that formed part of the Matter of Britain concerning the early Celtic British King Cunobeline. Although listed as a tragedy in the First Folio, modern critics often classify Cymbeline as a romance or even a comedy. Like Othello and The Winter's Tale, it deals with the themes of innocence and jealousy. While the precise date of composition remains unknown, the play was certainly produced as early as 1611.

Characters

In Britain

Cymbeline – King of Britain

Queen – Cymbeline's second wife

Imogen/Innogen – Cymbeline's daughter by a former queen, later disguised as the page Fidele

Posthumus Leonatus – Innogen's husband

Cloten – Queen's son by a former husband

Belarius – banished lord living under the name Morgan

Guiderius – Cymbeline's son, kidnapped in childhood by Belarius and raised as his son Polydore

Arvirargus – Cymbeline's son, kidnapped in childhood by Belarius and raised as his son Cadwal

Pisanio – Posthumus' servant

Cornelius – court physician

Helen – lady attending Imogen

Two Lords attending Cloten

Two Gentlemen

Two Captains

Two Jailers

In Rome

Philario – Posthumus' host in Rome

Iachimo/Giacomo – Philario's friend

French Gentleman

Dutch Gentleman
Spanish Gentleman
Caius Lucius – Roman ambassador and later general
Two Roman senators
Roman tribunes
Roman captain
Philharmonus – soothsayer
Apparitions
Jupiter – King of the Gods
Sicilius Leonatus – Posthumus' father
Posthumus' mother
Posthumus' two brothers

Synopsis

Cymbeline, the Roman Empire's vassal king of Britain, once had two sons, Guiderius and Arvirargus, but they were stolen twenty years earlier as infants by an exiled traitor named Belarius. Cymbeline now discovers that his only child left, his daughter Imogen (or Innogen), has secretly married her lover Posthumus Leonatus, an otherwise honourable man of Cymbeline's court. The lovers have exchanged jewellery as tokens: Imogen now with a bracelet, and Posthumus with a ring. Cymbeline dismisses the marriage and banishes Posthumus, since Imogen, as Cymbeline's only child, must produce a fully royal-blooded heir to succeed to the British throne. In the meantime, Cymbeline's Queen is conspiring to have Cloten, her cloddish and arrogant son by an earlier marriage, married to Imogen, to secure her bloodline. The Queen is also plotting to murder both Imogen and Cymbeline, procuring what she believes to be deadly poison from the court doctor, Cornelius, who, suspicious, switches the poison with a harmless sleeping potion. The Queen passes the "poison" along to Pisanio, Posthumus and Imogen's loving servant, who is led to believe it is a medicinal drug. No longer able to be with her banished Posthumus, Imogen secludes herself in her chambers, away from Cloten's aggressive advances.

Posthumus must now live in Italy, where he meets Iachimo (or Giacomo), who challenges the prideful Posthumus to a bet that he, Iachimo, can seduce Imogen, who Posthumus has praised for her chastity, and then bring Posthumus proof of Imogen's adultery. If Iachimo wins, he will get Posthumus's token ring. If Posthumus wins, not only must Iachimo pay him but also fight Posthumus in a duel with swords. Iachimo heads to Britain where he aggressively attempts to seduce the faithful Imogen, who sends him packing. Iachimo then hides in a chest in Imogen's bedchamber and, when the princess falls asleep, emerges to steal from her Posthumus's bracelet. He also takes note of the room and Imogen's partly naked body to be able to present false evidence to Posthumus that he has seduced his bride. Returning to Italy, Iachimo convinces Posthumus that he has successfully seduced Imogen. In his wrath, Posthumus sends two letters to Britain: one to Imogen, telling her to meet him at Milford Haven, on the Welsh coast; the other to the servant Pisanio, ordering him to murder Imogen at the Haven. However, Pisanio refuses to kill Imogen and reveals to her Posthumus's plot. He has Imogen disguise herself as a boy and continue to Milford Haven to seek employment. He also gives her the Queen's "poison," believing it will alleviate her psychological distress. In the guise of a boy, Imogen adopts the name "Fidele," meaning "faithful."

Back at Cymbeline's court, Cymbeline refuses to pay his British tribute to the Roman ambassador Caius Lucius, and Lucius warns Cymbeline of the Roman Emperor's forthcoming wrath, which will amount to an invasion of Britain by Roman troops. Meanwhile, Cloten learns of the "meeting" between Imogen and Posthumus at Milford Haven. Dressing himself enviously in Posthumus's clothes, he decides to go to Wales to kill Posthumus, and then rape, abduct, and marry Imogen. Imogen has now been travelling as "Fidele" through the Welsh mountains, her health in decline as she comes to a cave: the home of Belarius, along with his "sons" Polydore and Cadwal, whom he raised into great hunters. These two young men are in fact the British princes Guiderius and Arviragus, who themselves do not realise their own origin. The men discover "Fidele," and instantly captivated by a strange affinity for "him" become fast friends. Outside the cave, Guiderius is met by Cloten, who throws insults, leading to a sword fight during which Guiderius beheads Cloten. Meanwhile,

Imogen's fragile state worsens and she takes the "poison" as a hopeful medicine; when the men re-enter, they find her "dead." They mourn and, after placing Cloten's body beside hers, briefly depart to prepare for the double burial. Imogen awakes to find the headless body, and believes it to be Posthumus due to the fact the body is wearing Posthumus' clothes. Lucius' Roman soldiers have just arrived in Britain and, as the army moves through Wales, Lucius discovers the devastated "Fidele", who pretends to be a loyal servant grieving for his killed master; Lucius, moved by this faithfulness, enlists "Fidele" as a pageboy.

The treacherous Queen is now wasting away due to the disappearance of her son Cloten. Meanwhile, despairing of his life, a guilt-ridden Posthumus enlists in the Roman forces as they begin their invasion of Britain. Belarius, Guiderius, Arviragus, and Posthumus all help rescue Cymbeline from the Roman onslaught; the king does not yet recognise these four, yet takes notice of them as they go on to fight bravely and even capture the Roman commanders, Lucius and Iachimo, thus winning the day. Posthumus, allowing himself to be captured, as well as "Fidele", are imprisoned alongside the true Romans, all of whom await execution. In jail, Posthumus sleeps, while the ghosts of his dead family appear to complain to Jupiter of his grim fate. Jupiter himself then appears in thunder and glory to assure the others that destiny will grant happiness to Posthumus and Britain.

Cornelius arrives in the court to announce that the Queen has died suddenly, and that on her deathbed she unrepentantly confessed to villainous schemes against her husband and his throne. Both troubled and relieved at this news, Cymbeline prepares to execute his new prisoners, but pauses when he sees "Fidele," whom he finds both beautiful and somehow familiar. "Fidele" has noticed Posthumus' ring on Iachimo's finger and abruptly demands to know from where the jewel came. A remorseful Iachimo tells of his bet, and how he could not seduce Imogen, yet tricked Posthumus into thinking he had. Posthumus then comes forward to confirm Iachimo's story, revealing his identity and acknowledging his wrongfulness in desiring Imogen killed. Ecstatic, Imogen throws herself at Posthumus, who still takes her for a boy and knocks her down. Pisanio then rushes forward to explain that "Fidele" is Imogen in disguise; Imogen still suspects that Pisanio conspired with the Queen to give her the poison. Pisanio sincerely claims innocence, and Cornelius reveals how the poison was a non-fatal potion all along. Insisting that his betrayal years ago was a set-up, Belarius makes his own happy confession, revealing Guiderius and Arviragus as Cymbeline's own two long-lost sons. With her brothers restored to their place in the line of inheritance, Imogen is now free to marry Posthumus. An elated Cymbeline pardons Belarius and the Roman prisoners, including Lucius and Iachimo. Lucius calls forth his soothsayer to decipher a prophecy of recent events, which ensures happiness for all. Blaming his manipulative Queen for his refusal to pay earlier, Cymbeline now agrees to pay the tribute to the Roman Emperor as a gesture of peace between Britain and Rome, and he invites everyone to a great feast.

***** End of Plot Commentary *****

Look For Other Books Published By:
Literary Domain Publishing

NOTE: The printed books from ***Literary Domain Publishing*** are made on white quality paper with the size of 6x9 – the Shakespearan plays with a large font size of 12. Most of the books by ***Literary Domain Publishing*** are Public Domain and are "re-published" in order to make the books more readily available to the modern era. A commentary is usually supplied so a reader can quickly pre-view to see if it is worthwhile to invest the time in reading the book. It also gives an accurate book review by a qualified source or reader.

If there are other Public Domain books that you may wish to see in good quality printed form please let me know so that we can perhaps list it or publish it in the near future.

Contact me by email at:

peralta_mike@hotmail.com

LIFE CHANGING WORKS

The following books have deeply changed many lives. We list them here for your consideration.

The Bible both Old and New Testament. The best book as God never lies and He is never mistaken.

"The Rapture Was Real, And You Were Left Behind", and "Tethered: Survival Guide For Those Left Behind In The Tribulation" by Clare Dubois & Ezekiel Dubois. These books are filled with words of hope and instruction from the Lord Thy God as witnessed by one of His Brides. His words are the most valuable thing that we possess on Earth. There is no better book, besides the Holy Scriptures (Bible), to leave behind for your loved ones than this book. Do not take my word for it. Bring these most perfect teachings before the Lord in prayer and ask if they are truly from Him. You will get confirmation after confirmation as I and many others have. The Lord Jesus Christ is truly pouring out His Spirit right now. The doors of mercy are almost closed.

"Love Letters To My Bride 1, 2, &3" by Clare Dubois & Ezekiel Dubois. SO overwhelmed ... that I am at a loss to properly describe this book. Next to the Bible it is the most valuable message I have ever experienced in all of my life. It has caused me to finally overcome sins that have plagued me all my life – and it is His love that finally did it for me. Love never fails. Through this Jesus speaks to me directly. I hear His voice more clearly. I greatly encourage you to get a hold of these books. Through them you will hear Jesus' voice.

"Hell Testimonies" by Mike Peralta. This is a compilation of several Hell Testimonies from several people around the world. In my opinion this is the best book, after the Bible, (not because I'm the author) but because it mentions many types of sins that will send you to Hell. Some of the sins mentioned will probably hit home to you as you read this book. This book has helped me truly repent of sin more than any other book.

"While Out Of My Body I Saw God, Hell, and the Living Dead" by Dr. Roger Mills. This is a superb book about Hell. Jesus explains some things about Hell and sin that I have never read anywhere else. However, as far as I can see, it is all consistent with what the bible says.

"A Divine Revelation of Hell" by Mary Kathryn Baxter. This book shows in graphic detail what torment people in Hell are suffering. This book has been read by many and has helped many repent from their sins and obey God in their lives.

"Heaven Is So Real" by Choo Thomas. This book discusses both Heaven and Hell and reveals a great deal about the love and personality that Jesus has to His children as evidenced by how Jesus interacts with Choo Thomas. With a tenderness and friendly and loving and compassionate heart, you will learn the character and demeanor of Jesus through this book.

"Backsliding to Hell" by Mike Peralta. This book is written to help the backslider or those who are sinning after receiving Jesus in the past. It clearly explains through the Bible that the backslider will definitely go to Hell unless he or she repents of their sinning and turns back to Jesus. At first, to avoid promoting myself, I was not going to include this in my list of life changing books (truth2.weebly.com) but the Holy Spirit insisted that I include this book, so it must be even more important than I, myself, realize.

"Final Call, Exodus, My Son David, True Maturity" by Deborah Melissa Moller (Four Book Series). This four part series (combined in one book) has helped me more than any other book to get close to Jesus and obey God's will. It is like Jesus is personally teaching me how to follow Him, obey Him, love Him, and to do the Father's will. This is an extremely valuable book. It is truly a Pearl of Great Price. It is provided by Jesus to prepare His Bride for the very soon rapture.

Rapture and Tribulation books by Susan Davis: "Bride of Christ Prepare Now", "Left Behind After The Rapture", "Rapture or Tribulation", "Marriage Supper of the Lamb", "I Am Coming (Volumes 1 to 6)" by Susan Davis and Sabrina De Muynck. These rapture books are prophetic messages from Jesus to help prepare the Bride of Christ (Christ's true church) on how to prepare for the very soon rapture. It clearly shows that those who are not ready and are not looking to Jesus' soon coming will be left behind to face the anti-christ and certain death at the hands of the most ruthless evil dictator that will take power and world domination after the rapture. Also near the time of the rapture there will many deaths and those who are not ready will end up in Hell.

Links to rapture books are also at:
truth2.weebly.com

I urge you to read all these books – especially the Bible – over and over again. There is extremely little time left to get right with God. Jesus is returning much sooner than you think and there is soon to be terrible judgments on earth.

Surrender your life completely to Jesus now.

It is extremely and eternally dangerous to delay your full and absolute commitment to Christ. It doesn't matter what anyone else tells you – they cannot help you when you end up in Hell. Trust only God. Of course, love and pray for everyone – but trust only God.

Seek Him with all your being now before it's too late.

Feel free to email me at:
peralta_mike@hotmail.com

37359543R00102

Made in the USA
Middletown, DE
25 February 2019